Odd
EARL
Out

ANNA BRADLEY

OLIVER
HEBER
BOOKS

"You—you alone will have stars as no one else has them...You—only you will have stars that can laugh."

— ANTOINE DE SAINT-EXUPERY, *THE LITTLE PRINCE*

For my niece, Cora.

CHAPTER
ONE

L ord Barnaby was wearing a gold silk waistcoat embroidered with a dizzying array of green and blue... butterflies? Or were they flowers? Feathers, perhaps?

Miles Winthrop, the Earl of Cross and Lord Barnaby's much older and wiser cousin, squinted at the offensive garment. A gentleman's waistcoat was no place for flora and fauna, but butterflies would be better than...

"Dear God, Barnaby, are those *peacocks* embroidered on your waistcoat?"

"Peacocks!" Lord Barnaby shouted to be heard above the wind. "Don't be absurd, Cross. Do you think I'd wear a waistcoat covered with peacocks?"

If ever there were a question best left unanswered, it was that one.

Shiny, befeathered birds would be a grave assault on both his sartorial and ocular sensibilities, but he knew his cousin too well to be entirely easy on the subject of waistcoats, and they did look very much like—

"They're not *peacocks*, Cross." Barnaby wagged his

1

head like a dog, spraying a shower of water in every direction. "Why, anyone can see they're hummingbirds."

"Hummingbirds." Barnaby had worn a gold silk waistcoat embroidered with *hummingbirds* on a cold, wet ride through the mud and muck of the Oxfordshire countryside?

"Yes, hummingbirds. Peacocks, indeed. Really, Cross, do you suppose I wish to look like a fool?"

Alas, Barnaby hadn't sidestepped *that* quagmire as thoroughly as he seemed to think. "Of course, you're right, cousin. Every gentleman of taste must agree, hummingbirds are the pinnacle of restraint."

Fortunately, the waistcoat wasn't likely to survive the fury raining down on their heads. Dark clouds had been scudding across the sky when they'd left Steeple Cross earlier this afternoon, but the wind was now howling in earnest, and in the last hour the cold drizzle had become a relentless, driving rain that battered his skin with a thousand sharp pin pricks.

"You're drier than cinders, Cross." Barnaby let out one of the easy laughs that made him such a favorite among his friends. "I can't imagine why everyone in London complains of your dourness. I find you quite amusing, really."

"You're one of few, I assure you." Most of London found him grim enough. Of course, that hadn't stopped any of them from accepting an invitation to his hunting party, had it? Aristocrats were nothing if not opportunistic.

"What happened to the scarlet waistcoat with the gold-embroidered suns I sent you last month?" Barnaby asked. "I haven't seen you wear it once. You're an unrelenting parade of dark blue, brown, and black wool. A touch of color would do you a world of good."

"Blue, brown, and black *are* colors, Barnaby." Miles flicked a spot of mud from the sleeve of his navy riding coat.

"Not nice ones. What's wrong with the scarlet waistcoat? Indeed, Cross, the suns are exquisitely done. You won't find better suns in all of Bond Street."

"I believe Vincent took it off somewhere." His valet, Vincent, was a slavish devotee of the Beau Brummel school of fashion. He'd taken one look at the sun-bedecked scarlet monstrosity, shuddered visibly, and consigned it to the deepest depths of the wardrobe.

Miles hadn't seen it since, which was just as well.

"There's nothing wrong with a bit of whimsy now and then." Barnaby eyed Miles's dark gray waistcoat with the plain silver buttons, his nose wrinkling. "Really, Cross. I don't know why you always insist on dressing as if you're in mourning."

It was a great pity he *wasn't* in mourning, as it would have given him the perfect excuse to cancel this house party, but there weren't any Winthrops left to die. He and Barnaby were the only two left.

In any case, it was too late. Half the *ton* had already arrived, and the other half was scurrying across Oxfordshire toward Steeple Cross even now, the gentlemen salivating at the promise of lively sport, lavish dinners, and excellent port, and the ladies plotting the usual romantic intrigues that were the bane of every house party.

It was a damnable way to spend a fortnight. He despised romantic intrigues with the same virulent loathing Vincent reserved for vulgar waistcoats, but a man must endure all manner of unpleasant things, particularly when he was an earl in need of an heir.

"Brightly-embroidered waistcoats are all the rage in London this season, Cross. Every gentleman of fashion is wearing them."

"Every dandy, you mean." Was Barnaby a Bond Street Beaux now? Good Lord, he hoped not, but the hummingbirds weren't reassuring.

"Not *just* the dandies."

"You forget I spent time in London this season, cousin." More time than he'd ever cared to, every second of which he heartily regretted. "I didn't see a single gentleman of any sense wearing a waistcoat embroidered with peacocks."

Plenty of fools, though. There was no shortage of those in London.

"Hummingbirds, Cross, *hummingbirds*, and I saw Lord Arthur wearing an embroidered silk waistcoat at Lord Babbage's rout just a few weeks ago."

"I do hope you're not holding Lord Arthur up as a paragon of good sense. The man is as penetrating as a blade of grass."

"If that, but he's good fun. Did you invite him to Steeple Cross?"

"No, but there will be enough people milling about to keep you entertained." Fortunately, Steeple Cross was more of a country estate than a gentleman's hunting box, and could accommodate a large party.

Or was that unfortunate? He could no longer tell.

"What people?" Barnaby made a face. "Not those dullards from the Royal Society, I hope."

"Everyone." It wasn't as much of an exaggeration

as he wished, God help him. "Your old companions from Oxford. Lord and Lady Kimble and their three daughters, Lord Ambrose and his daughter, Lady Cecil and her nieces, and a few dozen others from that set."

"Why so many daughters and nieces? We'll be overrun with ladies!"

That was rather the point, but Barnaby would discover what was in store for him soon enough without Miles hurrying him along. "Lady Fosberry will be here, and Lady Drummond. You remember Lady Drummond and her daughter, Lady Cora?"

Barnaby and Lady Cora had grown up in the same neighborhood in Hereford. They were close in age, and had been friendly as children.

"Vaguely, yes." Barnaby shrugged with an indifference that would not have endeared him to the young lady in question. "How does she do?"

"Very well, from what I understand."

"You didn't see her in London?"

"No, just Lady Drummond, but she tells me Lady Cora has grown into a lovely, elegant young lady." Hopefully Lady Drummond hadn't exaggerated her daughter's appeal, as he had no patience for giggling schoolgirls.

Barnaby snorted. "Her *mother* says so? Everyone knows you can't believe what the mother says, Cross. I remember Lady Cora as a scrawny chit with yellow hair."

A scrawny chit with yellow hair? Good Lord. That sounded like the sort of unkind, ruthlessly accurate comment Miles's father might have made. Barnaby was the heart of amiability, but the Cross blood did rear its ugly head now and again. "I hope to God you

5

have the sense not to repeat such a comment in Lady Cora's hearing."

Or in any young lady's hearing, or this thing would be over before it began.

"Lady Cora must be... what? Eighteen or nineteen years old now? Why wasn't she in London for the season with her mother?" Barnaby's brows lowered, as if Lady Cora's absence must be the result of some deep, dark secret. "Why didn't she debut?"

"Lady Drummond's father passed away just before Christmas last year, and she and Lady Cora are only recently out of mourning. Lady Drummond was in London to see to some business, not for the season."

"I can't imagine Lady Cora is keen on grouse hunting." The wind tried to send Barnaby's hat whirling into the tempest, but he snatched it back and jammed it down onto his head. "She used to be fond of flowers and smallish animals, if I recall. She was forever running off to the stables to play with the kittens."

"Flowers and kittens? What a disagreeable sounding child." Whatever she'd once been, Lady Cora was now an appropriate and eligible young lady, and that was enough to secure her an invitation to Steeple Cross.

"I hope you haven't invited too many ladies, Cross. They'll interfere with our sport. I don't fancy hanging about the house all day, drinking tea."

"Come, Barnaby. Have you ever heard of a hunting party without sport?"

But there would be tea as well, and dinners, and interminable hours spent in the drawing room listening to one young lady or other laboring over the pianoforte, and a number of other unpleasant things, because the Cross earldom must have an heir.

A *legitimate* heir.

One needed a wife for that. So, Steeple Cross was to be overrun with a herd of young ladies for the next fortnight, all of them suitably marriageable.

Any one of them would do for Barnaby.

As for Lady Cora Drummond's scrawniness and yellow hair, a few years could work wonders in a young lady's appearance. There was every reason to hope her sharp angles had turned curvy, and her yellow hair had mellowed to a soft gold.

Barnaby was fond of gold, if one could judge by his waistcoat.

"I was surprised to hear *you* were in London for the season, Cross." Barnaby cast him a sly look from the corner of his eye. "A bit out of character, isn't it?"

Of course, his cousin had heard, because as dour and dull as Miles was, his name still found its way to every rumormonger's lips sooner or later, and this season more than ever before. "The gossips in London are as busy as ever, I see."

"Always. They never cease, and you *are* an earl, after all. No doubt they all believed you'd come to London on the hunt for a countess. What a pity you didn't find her while you were there."

A memory tried to creep in then, of laughing red lips and sparkling dark blue eyes set like jewels in the face of a lady with sleek, silky hair as dark as midnight, but Miles shut it out before her features could fully emerge from the shadows of his mind. "I wasn't on the hunt for a countess. I promised Melrose I would accompany him to London for a season, and I did. That's all."

"You can't put marrying off forever, Cross."

Certainly, he could. If nothing else, his adventures this season had confirmed what he'd suspected all along.

He wasn't *ever* going to marry.

No doubt that news would devastate London's eligible young ladies, but—

"How old are you now, Cross? Forty? Forty-one?"

"*Forty-one*! I'm twenty-nine, for God's sake."

"What, is that all? I beg your pardon." Barnaby's eyes were dancing with laughter. "I had you at a mere handful of years away from your dotage."

Impudent pup. "You're a great nuisance, Barnaby, and not nearly as clever as you fancy yourself to be."

Barnaby snorted. "Well, no, but only because I fancy myself very clever, indeed."

"You'll marry before I do." The sooner Barnaby succumbed to the parson's mousetrap, the more comfortably Miles could rest at night.

Since he'd inherited the viscountcy two years earlier, Barnaby had taken to gadding about London with a group of fashionable scoundrels who had far fewer scruples than they did gold coins in their pockets. A tidy fortune had come with Barnaby's title, but profligacy would put an end to it quickly enough.

Yet Barnaby had a great many admirable qualities, and might yet make an acceptable Earl of Cross one day, if he didn't ruin himself first with drink and debts.

He'd need to be properly managed, however.

But to conjure an acceptable earl from the ashes of a rogue, one first required an admirable countess. Hence the stable of eager young ladies even now assembling at Steeple Cross.

"I do hope you aren't scheming to marry me off, Cross." Barnaby let out the carefree chuckle of a man who hadn't any idea of the nefarious plans in store for him. "I came to hunt grouse, not wives."

"There's no reason you can't hunt both, is there? Any one of the young ladies attending the house party would make a proper wife for you, Barnaby."

Barnaby's grin faded, replaced by a look of dawning horror. "Good Lord. Please tell me that isn't why you've invited them all to Steeple Cross!"

"I invited them because that's what one does when one has a house party." It was the truth, or most of it. As for the *rest* of the truth, it would out soon enough, but this wasn't the proper time to make a full confession, or Barnaby would almost certainly become contrary.

Countesses were a delicate business. One must tread lightly.

"Bloody good thing, Cross, because I have no desire to marry yet, and even if I did, I wouldn't choose Lady Cora Drummond. We were friends a long time ago, and we're not anything anymore."

"Friends become lovers all the time, Barnaby. Who better to marry than a lady you know, who was once your friend?"

"Why, a lady I'm in love with, of course!" Barnaby flung his arms out wide, his reins dangling from his fingers. "Nothing less than love could *ever* compel me to marry."

Ah, spoken like a passionate young man. Had he ever been as passionate as that? He'd certainly never been so young. "It pains me to shatter your illusions, cousin, but love has made far more men miserable than happy. You're better off marrying a lady you ad-

9

mire and respect than one you've lost your head over."

"Why can't I have a lady I admire, respect, *and* am madly in love with?" Barnaby didn't wait for an answer, but tapped his heels into his horse's flanks and shot forward, heedless of the muck flying from the beast's hooves.

But it would take more than a bit of mud to end this discussion. Miles went after his cousin, and caught him at the crest of a rise, his horse's hooves skidding in the deep muck. "No man gets everything he desires in a wife, Barnaby."

"Bollocks."

"The idea that there is a lady out there more perfect for us than any other, a lady who calls forth all our tender sentiments, a lady who stirs our mind as well as our loins is an illusion, cousin."

"*Loins?* For God's sake, Cross."

"There is no such lady for you." Nor was there any such lady for *him*. There was *no* lady for him at all, come to that. If he'd briefly thought otherwise, it had only been very briefly, and that madness had thankfully passed—

"What the devil is that?" Barnaby was peering over Miles's shoulder.

"What are loins? I'd think you'd know that by now." Barnaby had gone to Eton, after all.

Barnaby blinked, then swiped his arm across his eyes. "It looks like—"

"I know what loins look like, cousin. There's no need for an anatomy lesson."

"For God's sake, Cross, not loins! *That!*" Barnaby pointed toward a thick grove of trees at the edge of the field. "Do you see those tracks in the mud?"

"I see them." The long, jagged furrows cut deep into the soaked ground were the exact shape and width of carriage wheels, and they led to a wide gap in the tree line that was surrounded by broken branches.

A carriage had slid sideways off the road and into the trees.

Miles stilled, but the only sound was the ceaseless pounding of the rain. Steely gray clouds had massed to the east, bleak shadows against the backdrop of a foreboding sky, almost like a warning, a sign of bad luck to come. "Quickly, Barnaby. There's a hill on the other side of those trees. If the carriage slid too far, they may have gone over the edge."

He jerked on the reins, harness jingling as his horse gave a protesting toss of her head, and then he was off, Barnaby charging after him.

CHAPTER
TWO

Juliet Templeton didn't believe in bad luck.

Black cats had never troubled her. Down-turned horseshoes didn't give her palpitations, nor did she fall into fits of despair over cracked looking glasses. At the advanced age of twenty-one—an age at which a lady was said by some to be hovering on the verge of spinsterhood—she'd yet to experience an honest-to-goodness harbinger of doom.

Dire forebodings, ill omens and threatening signs were for the feeble-minded, not for ladies who could recite every word of Shakespeare's *Romeo and Juliet* from memory.

But if she *had* believed in such things, she might be a trifle worried right now.

"I don't like to be grim, dearest, but I can't help but think we made a dreadful mistake leaving Fowler behind at the Fox Inn with the carriage. He... oh, my goodness!" They pitched sideways, and Lady Fosberry was obliged to grab Juliet's arm to keep from tumbling off the bench. "Now this other scoundrel has run off, and left two defenseless ladies alone in the wilderness to face whatever tragedy befalls us!"

Defenseless? Hardly, but poor Lady Fosberry had gone rather shrill, so it didn't seem an appropriate time to quibble over adjectives. "Nonsense, my lady! Why, I'm certain he's on his way back to us even now."

He *wasn't* on his way back. Not now, and not ever.

He being their hired driver, who'd leapt from the box of the disabled carriage hours ago, swearing he'd find his way to Steeple Cross and fetch help. Instead, he'd released the horse from its traces, mounted it, and promptly vanished into the night like an apparition.

"Fowler told me he was well enough to make it another ten miles, and I daresay I should have listened to him. He never would have left us in such a dreadful predicament."

"Oh, come now, my lady. It's not as dreadful as you make it out to be."

It *was* as dreadful as her ladyship made it out to be, and worse besides.

The trip from London had begun delightfully enough. They'd passed the time in pleasant chatter, interspersed with an occasional snooze on Lady Fosberry's part.

If Juliet *had* occasionally been troubled by a pang of misgiving about what might await her at Lord Cross's house party, it was easy enough to dismiss it while the sun was shining, and endless green hills were rolling by outside the carriage window.

But as soon as they ventured into Oxfordshire, the heavens had opened with a vengeance, battering the roof of the carriage and pummeling Fowler, Lady Fosberry's driver, with such unrelenting fury the poor man had been feverish by the time they'd reached Chipping Norton.

So, they'd gone on, entrusting themselves to a hired driver for the last ten miles of their journey, leaving Fowler at The Fox to rest until he felt well enough to come to Steeple Cross with the carriage.

That had been their first mistake, and rather an egregious one, as it turned out.

Since then, the calamities had multiplied with alarming rapidity, until they were beset on every side. One of their wheels was sunk deep in the mud, the rain had reached biblical levels of fury, dark was descending upon them, and the wind was threatening to tear the doors right off the carriage.

Really, it was enough to make a lady doubt her decisions.

But it wasn't as if some hulking villain had come lurching out of the darkness, pistol in hand, and threatened their lives. As bad as their predicament was, it couldn't properly be termed a harbinger of doom without a highwayman, could it? Unless a highwayman appeared, she refused to believe the elements had conspired to punish them.

Well, it would either be a highwayman, or—

Crack!

The carriage rocked, throwing Juliet up against the door. Lady Fosberry bounced on the cushions, but managed to stay upright by clutching at Juliet as if she were a cricket bat. Three or four bone-jarring bumps followed, before the carriage at last shuddered to a halt.

"Oh, my goodness! Juliet, are you hurt, child? Dear God, what happened? I thought we were stuck in the mud!"

Not any longer, it seemed. Their carriage had just plummeted a half-dozen feet, and was now listing heavily to one side. If it wasn't *quite* a harbinger of doom, it was certainly concerning.

Juliet struggled to her knees and peered out the window. It was late afternoon, but the sky was so dark with ominous black clouds it might as well have been midnight. Everything was distorted with sheets of rain, but the shadowy lumps surrounding them were presumably trees, the black pit beneath them an ocean of mud, and the edge where the ground dropped steeply away...

Oh. The hired coachman's defection made a lot more sense *now*.

They were stuck on the side of a hill, with two of the carriage wheels already over the edge. The only reason they hadn't plunged to their doom was that the wheels were buried deep in the mud.

The hill wasn't a terribly steep one, but steep enough that if they slid any farther the carriage would overturn, toppling them roof over axle, and they *would* slide farther, as the rain continued to wash away the mud under their wheels.

It was another disaster in the making, but she wouldn't give it a chance to strike. Sometimes a lady had to make her own luck, and this was one of those times. "Now then, my lady. I'm afraid we'll have to walk the rest of the way to Steeple Cross."

Lady Fosberry stared at her, aghast. "You mean for us to go wandering about the countryside on foot?"

"The landlady at The Fox said Steeple Cross isn't more than ten miles east of Chipping Norton, and we've done eight miles of that already." Her calculations might be just a *touch* optimistic, but it couldn't be more than a three-mile walk from here to Steeple Cross.

Certainly, no more than four.

"But you just told me our driver was likely on his way back to us!"

"Yes, well, I may have been mistaken." She hadn't *lied*, of course. Nothing so dishonest as that. She hadn't precisely told the truth, either, but this was no time to quibble over verbs any more than it was adjectives.

"Here, my lady, slide to the other side of the seat, won't you?" Juliet helped Lady Fosberry wriggle to the middle of the bench, then crawled over her on her hands and knees to the door. "Now, I'm just going to pop out there, and then I'll reach in and help you out, all right?"

"Out? Oh, dear. *Outside*, in this weather! We'll both be soaked to the skin!"

Better soaked than tumbled head over heels to the bottom of a hill and trapped inside a wrecked carriage, but there was no need to rattle poor Lady Fosberry further by being so brutally descriptive. "I'm afraid so, yes. The carriage isn't quite steady, you see, and I don't like for you to be jostled about."

Or hurled out a window like a ragdoll.

Lady Fosberry cast an anxious look over her shoulder at the opposite window, then turned back to Juliet with a nod. "Yes, all right."

"Good. Now, keep still for just a moment, my lady."

It took a good deal of shimmying and squirming to get the door open at such an awkward angle, and even more to wriggle her way out of it, but she managed it, and was able to hold the door open for Lady Fosberry and help her out of the carriage. "Mind the edge, my lady. We can't have you toppling down the hill, can we? There, that's very good."

"Good, is it? I admire your pluck, dearest, but I confess I find it difficult to be optimistic when I'm ankle deep in mud."

It wasn't just any mud either, but cold, slippery Oxfordshire mud, the sort that sucked at one's feet with every step. "I'm certain the road will be better."

But the road—if you could call it a road at all, which she didn't—*wasn't* better. It was more a torrent of mud with bits of higher ground visible here and there, like lily pads atop a pond.

Except instead of a pond, it was a deluge.

Dear God, how in the world could her ladyship make her way through it?

The answer was plain. She *couldn't.*

Yet the mere idea of the alternative, leaving Lady Fosberry here alone while she went off to fetch help was so unbearable, it made Juliet's heart plummet.

Oh, *how* had things come to such a catastrophic pass as this?

But there was no use bemoaning her fate, as it was, alas, sealed. She glanced up at the menacing sky, her heart thudding in time with the pelting rain, the darkness pressing in on her, her ears ringing from the merciless roar of the wind.

"Juliet? You look positively despairing, dearest. I don't imagine we're in for a pleasant walk, but we'll muddle through some—"

"No." Juliet caught Lady Fosberry's hands in a desperate squeeze. "I think... I think it would be best if you waited here, my lady, and I went on my own."

18

"Certainly not! Why, it's out of the question. Indeed, Juliet, I forbid it!"

"I'm afraid we haven't much choice, my lady. Surely, you must see that?"

"But you can't just go wandering about in the dark alone! It isn't..." Lady Fosberry's hands fluttered as she searched for the proper word.

Safe? Rational? Sane? Sadly, any one of those would do. "It isn't what?"

"It isn't ladylike!"

Ladylike? Juliet opened her mouth, and amazingly, a choked laugh emerged. It did, admittedly, sound a trifle unhinged, but a laugh was a laugh, even if it was tinged with hysteria.

After a moment of startled silence, Lady Fosberry let out a forlorn chuckle. "I suppose propriety is the least of our worries now, isn't it?"

"I'm afraid so." Juliet had never been much concerned with propriety to begin with. What was the use? She wasn't a titled lady, an heiress, or even fashionable, and her mother had seen to it not a single aristocrat in London ever said the name Templeton without a snicker or a gasp.

And that was *before* this season's scandal.

"I'd best get on my way, while the daylight still holds." The daylight in this case was as dark as the deepest pit of Hades, but she couldn't delay. Everyone knew disasters always struck in the dead of night.

"Oh, dear. I don't like this, Juliet. What if you get lost? How will I ever find you?"

"I won't leave the road, my lady. I promise it." The landlady at The Fox had told them Steeple Cross was visible from the road. As long as she didn't wander off course, she'd stumble upon it sooner or later.

"You will be careful, won't you? Your sisters will never forgive me if I lose you somewhere in Oxfordshire."

"I'll never forgive you, either. If I must be lost forever, I prefer it to happen in London, preferably somewhere near Gunter's." She grinned at Lady Fosberry, then turned to set off down the road, but she hadn't taken two steps before she turned back again.

Lady Fosberry was huddled under a tree, rain dripping from the brim of her ruined straw hat, looking so small, wet, and *alone*, Juliet couldn't force her feet to take another step. Lady Fosberry had been such a good friend to her father, and to all of them. Surely, she deserved better than to be left here in the dark in the wilds of Oxfordshire, at the mercy of the elements and whatever vicious animals were lurking nearby? And what of the highwaymen? This road was notorious for them, and though none had yet appeared, with the way things were going, it was only a matter of time before gangs of them emerged from the darkness.

She hurried back the way she'd come. "Does Fowler keep a pistol, my lady?"

Lady Fosberry blinked. "Who do you intend to shoot?"

"No one, hopefully, as I'd really rather not, but I'd feel ever so much better leaving you here if I knew you had a pistol."

"Fowler keeps a brace of them, yes, but I'm afraid..." Lady Fosberry cast a stricken glance behind her at the carriage. "He hid them behind the driver's box before we left The Fox."

"The driver's box." Of *course*, that's where they'd be, because the box was the one place she couldn't reach from the ground. As if a furious storm, a cowardly driver, a carriage accident, and roving bands of brutal highwaymen weren't enough of a challenge, now she'd have to climb on top of a carriage listing so heavily to one side it looked like a turtle toppled over onto its back.

But there was no use fuming over it, and it was her own fault, for not thinking of the pistols sooner. "Right. I'll just fetch them, shall I?"

Juliet didn't give Lady Fosberry a chance to object. She hurried to the carriage, grasped the top edge of one of the wheels and hauled herself up, her feet slipping over the muddy hub. She was able to drag herself over the wheel and squeeze into the narrow space behind the driver's box, but the carriage rocked, as if making up its mind whether to remain upright or tumble down the hill, and there was an ominous crack, like wood snapping.

"Juliet!" Lady Fosberry's terrified shriek rent the air. "One of the wheel's spokes has snapped!"

Juliet widened her stance and grabbed the back of the driver's seat, bracing herself, though neither would do the least bit of good if the carriage went over the edge.

Crack!

"Oh, my goodness! We've lost another spoke. Don't move, dearest!"

Juliet froze—everything but her heart, which was kicking up enough of a fuss to send the whole equipage lurching down the side of the hill. Even now she could feel the carriage shuddering around her, as if it were readying itself for its inevitable demise. "Where are the pistols?"

"Never mind the blasted pistols! Come down from there at once before you—"

Crack!

"God in heaven! Jump, dearest! Quickly!"

Jump? The very thought of leaping into the darkness froze her blood to ice. "You just told me not to move!" Surely, there must be another way?

"Yes, but I'm afraid... well, you're going to end up on the ground one way or another, aren't you? Better here than at the bottom of the hill! Just, er, make certain you leap as far wide of the carriage as you can, as the jolt is sure to send it careening over the edge."

Was that meant to be reassuring? Because it wasn't, at all.

Juliet peered over the side of the carriage—a mistake, as the ground seemed much further away than it had when she'd climbed up, but Lady Fosberry was right—it was a great deal closer than the ground at the bottom of the hill.

Well, then. That answered that question, didn't it? "Stay back, my lady. I'm coming down!"

"Wait!" Lady Fosberry was babbling something, a stream of incoherent words in a shrill, piercing shriek that carried through the darkness, but her voice was drowned out by another noise—the sound of a horse's heavy snort, the squelch of hooves in the mud and... men, shouting?

Juliet wiped the rain from her eyes and squinted into the darkness, but once again a swatch of unremitting black met her eyes. Had someone come? Or, dear God, was she becoming delusional, like poor King Lear?

She crept closer to the edge, one tiny movement at a time, her heart pounding against her ribs at every infinitesimal shift of the carriage beneath her, until at last she was clear of the wheel, with nothing standing between her and the ground but...

Air. Empty, gaping, yawning space, a bottomless chasm.

Sweat trickled from her temple, and her hands... what was wrong with her hands? Her fingers and toes were tingling, her knees shaking, and her head, well, it didn't feel right. It was too light for her body, and swimming with dizziness.

Oh, but heights were dreadful, terrible things! She'd never liked them, and she liked them even less in the dark, but the ground must be down there somewhere, mustn't it? Just because she couldn't see it didn't mean she was about to leap into an abyss.

Did it?

"Wait, Juliet! Just another moment—"

Lady Fosberry was cut off by another sickening crack.

Was that the third spoke snapping, or the fourth? She'd lost count, but by the time she'd drawn another shuddering breath, it no longer mattered. The floor tilted, and then with a final terrifying groan, the carriage vanished from underneath her feet. She let out a breathless cry, cold rain flooding her mouth and numbing her tongue, but the wailing wind snatched it, and snuffed it into silence.

For an instant she seemed to hang in mid-air, legs flailing uselessly, black stars—was there such a thing? bursting at the edges of her vision, then she was falling, her lungs grasping uselessly for air, the ground rushing up to meet her. She squeezed her eyes shut, shattered bones and pools of blood etched on her eyelids...

But the ground wasn't *there*. Something else was in its place, something quick and powerful that plucked her from the darkness, closed around her like a vice, and jerked her from mid-air into a hard, solid wall.

"Juliet!" It was Lady Fosberry's voice, high-pitched with fright. "Is she hurt?"

Was she hurt? She hardly knew. She tried to answer, to reassure her ladyship, but her mouth was clumsy, the words tangling in her tongue, and she couldn't hear herself over the wind and the roar of blood in her ears, or see through the darkness and the streaks of rain in her eyes, and she was tired, so tired, her limbs weighted, sinking...

Then, blessed silence.

When she woke again, the wind was whipping around her in driving sheets, and water was trickling in icy rivulets down the back of her neck, but she was huddled inside something warm, and surrounded by the rich, dark scent of it.

A horse swayed beneath her, a pair of large, long-fingered hands gripped the reins in front of her, and Lord Cross's voice murmured in her ear, his warm breath drifting over her neck, "Welcome to Steeple Cross, Miss Templeton."

CHAPTER
THREE

One moment Miles was riding through the trees, squinting against the torrent of rain blasting into his face, and the next, a cold, wet, squirming lady had tumbled from the sky, and fallen right into his arms.

A second lady darted from the trees, streaks of mud and a bedraggled hat obscuring her face, but he would have known Lady Fosberry anywhere. "My lady, are you—"

"Juliet!" Lady Fosberry rushed toward him, features twisted and her face white with panic. "Is she hurt?"

Juliet? Surely, she didn't mean...

But even before he glanced down at the lady in his arms, he knew he'd find *her* face—the firm, dimpled chin and the full, red lips that seemed always on the verge of a teasing smile.

No. God in heaven, *no.*

Juliet Templeton, one of the few ladies who'd ever dared to tease *him.* But her lips were silent now, her eyelids fluttering over closed eyes, her skin pale and colder than ice.

"By Gad, Cross, that was well done, but we've no time to crown you with laurels just yet. These ladies are half drowned as it is." Barnaby didn't wait for an answer, but leapt from his horse's back and assisted Lady Fosberry into the saddle before remounting, and winding his way through the trees to what was left of the road.

The sky was completely dark now, the last feeble glow extinguished by the storm, but Miles knew every inch of his property, down to each stone and rut in the road. He took the lead, and it wasn't long before Steeple Cross emerged from the darkness. The entire ground floor was ablaze with light, and several elegant equipages were stopped at the top of the drive, a flurry of activity surrounding them.

Another crowd of guests had just arrived, despite the foul weather, but instead of meeting them with the dignity that befitted a host, he'd be doing so with a Juliet-Templeton-shaped mud print smeared across the front of his best riding coat.

But short of stashing her in the stables, there was nothing to be done.

Every head turned toward them as he led the pitiful little parade of four into the entryway, trailing an ocean of mud and wet behind them. His house-keeper, Mrs. Poole let out a quiet gasp at the sight of them, and one of Lady Cecil's nieces tittered, then slapped a hand over her mouth.

Any other lady would have been mortified to appear in his entryway looking like a nightmarish amalgamation of a street urchin, a chimney sweep, and a drowned cat.

But not Juliet Templeton.

She was in a shocking state, her hair hanging in a

26

sopping, tangled mess down her back. Her hat was gone, only a bit of straw and limp ribbon left to attest to its ever having been there at all, and the hems of her skirts were so encrusted with muck she left a dark streak on the immaculate, black-and-white checkered marble floor behind her.

Yet still, somehow, she managed to look as if she were right where she belonged, as if she'd intended from the start to be caught in a torrential downpour, narrowly avoid a carriage accident, and appear before the company with mud streaking her face and wet leaves caught in her hair.

By now, he shouldn't even be surprised at it.

Nothing—not youth, inexperience, nor a scandal the likes of which London hadn't seen in decades seemed able to shake Juliet Templeton. Somehow, she contrived to always land on her feet.

Or, failing that, in his arms.

What in God's name was she *doing* here? Was she not satisfied with the havoc she'd wreaked in London, and now must have Oxfordshire, as well? Would that she'd kept far away from Steeple Cross.

Far away from him—

"And *whom*, Lord Cross, have we here?"

Lady Cecil, who'd just arrived with her two nieces and was following a housemaid up the staircase to their rooms, had paused on the first landing to stare down at Juliet, her long, thin nose twitching like an outraged rodent's.

She knew who Juliet was. After this season, everyone in London did. "I'm certain you must know Lady Fosberry, Lady Cecil, and this young lady is Miss Juliet Templeton."

Lady Cecil let out a theatrical gasp, and pressed a

shaking hand to her breast. "My goodness, Lord Cross! You invited *Miss Juliet Templeton* to your house party?"

He summoned the cool expression that had sent more than one lady scurrying across a ballroom to avoid him. "I should think that was obvious, Lady Cecil, given she's standing right in front of you."

That he'd just been lamenting Juliet's presence at Steeple Cross only moments before didn't matter. He could be as contrary as he wished in his own house.

Lady Cecil seized each of her nieces by their wrists and jerked them behind her, as if they might be contaminated by breathing the same air as the notorious Miss Templeton. "You astonish me, Lord Cross."

"Not for the first time, I trust, or the last, but you needn't concern yourself with my guest list, my lady." He nodded at Sarah, one of his housemaids, who was hovering over Lady Cecil's shoulder. "I'm afraid you're overset with fatigue, Lady Cecil. Do feel at liberty to retire. Sarah will show you and your nieces to your rooms."

He watched Lady Cecil flounce up the stairs, calling a pox down on her head for forcing him into such a fit of gallantry. He hadn't done it for Juliet Templeton's sake, of course—God knew he had no desire to justify her presence here.

No, it was the poor sportsmanship of the thing that irritated him. Juliet had no other defenders, as Barnaby had hurried Lady Fosberry down the hallway to Miles's study, and she couldn't properly defend herself, with her teeth chattering as they were.

Lady Cecil was like a cobra, sinking her poisonous fangs into an injured rabbit.

Then again, there was nothing feeble about Juliet. Somehow, she even managed to *drip* charmingly, the widening puddle surrounding her lapping gently at the toes of her half-boots, like a devoted dog begging for any errant crumbs of her attention.

The sooner he whisked her out of sight, the less of an uproar her presence would cause. If any of Barnaby's roguish friends happened by, they'd be groveling at her feet soon enough as well, and no end of trouble would follow. Men tended to lose their wits around Juliet Templeton, and Barnaby's companions had few enough wits to spare as it was.

But she'd be gone soon enough, and he could begin the process of putting her out of his mind. Or resume it, rather, as he hadn't managed to forget her for more than two minutes at a time since their first fateful meeting six weeks earlier, despite a humiliatingly vigorous attempt to do so.

"Come with me, Miss Templeton." He marched down the hallway, sidestepping the stream of muddy sludge Barnaby and Lady Fosberry had left in their wake. He didn't look at her again, but he could hear the wet squeak of her boots and the soggy drag of her skirts behind him.

They met Barnaby coming out of the study. "Ah, Cross, there you are. I've just left Lady Fosberry in her bedchamber, and ordered a bath brought up for her. May I take you up as well, Miss Templeton?"

Miles didn't give her a chance to reply. "Not just yet, Barnaby. I'd like a word with Miss Templeton first."

"For God's sake, Cross, she'll catch her death—"

"It's quite all right, Lord Barnaby." Juliet gave him

a warm smile. "I thank you for your assistance with Lady Fosberry."

"My pleasure, Miss Templeton." Barnaby bowed, then drew Miles aside and muttered, "I can't imagine what you need to say to Miss Templeton that can't wait until tomorrow, Cross, but do behave yourself, won't you?"

"I think I can be trusted not to behave like an utter savage in my own study." He pushed Barnaby out the door, closing it on his cousin's warning look, and turned his attention to Juliet. "Well, Miss Templeton. You certainly know how to make an entrance."

It hadn't sounded like an accusation in his head, but the words fell between them with an edge so sharp and flinty, it might have sliced through bone.

If Juliet noticed it, it didn't dim the smile she gave him, the one that drew his gaze to her lips like a starving man to a feast. "Lady Cecil thought so."

She had, indeed, and Lady Cecil, for all her ill-tempered arrogance, had been perfectly correct about Juliet's presence here. "Lord Barnaby tells me your driver left you and Lady Fosberry stranded on the road."

"Yes, I'm afraid he abandoned us as soon as he realized the carriage was in danger of tumbling down the hill. I can't say how grateful I am for your assistance, my lord. I don't know how you managed to catch me, but I might have broken my neck, but for you."

It was a pretty speech, but he waved her thanks aside with a sweep of his hand. He didn't want or need anything from her, aside from her absence from his home.

But he was a gentleman, and gentlemen didn't toss young ladies out of their houses in middle of the night after they'd nearly tumbled over the edge of a cliff.

No matter how much they might wish to.

"May I offer you a splash of port, Miss Templeton?" Yes, that was very good. Courteous, even solicitous. He'd have no reason to reproach himself for his behavior once she was gone.

She smiled that smile again, like a flower bursting into bloom. "Is it *Miss Templeton* now? It was Miss Juliet before you left London."

Yes, he remembered, and he also remembered what followed. It was risky, calling her Juliet, because then he'd think of her as Juliet, and that sort of familiarity led to... inappropriate thoughts, to longing and yearning and aching, and all manner of other dangerous things.

"Are we no longer on such intimate terms as we once were, my lord?"

Miles fumbled with the bottle of port in his hand, the clink of glass loud in the quiet room. If they had been on intimate terms, then *intimacy* meant far less to her than it did to him.

Abruptly, he was deeply, hotly furious.

Since he'd arrived at Steeple Cross, he'd done everything he could do to forget her.

Her name, her face...

Now here she was again, her smile like a red cloak waved in the face of a charging bull.

It would take weeks for him to unsee that smile, weeks to unhear that soft, teasing voice, and longer still for him to banish the face it conjured. "We have *never* been on intimate terms, Miss Templeton. Indeed, I find myself at an utter loss to explain your presence at Steeple Cross."

Her mouth dropped open, and she flushed to the roots of her hair. "I don't understand, my lord. Lady Fosberry—"

"I didn't invite you here, so what in the world could have possessed you to appear on my doorstep?"

Good Lord, had he said that *aloud*?

Juliet Templeton had the widest, bluest eyes he'd ever seen, but somehow, incredibly, the damnable woman contrived to make them even wider and bluer. "You didn't invite me," she repeated, as if to be sure she'd heard him correctly. "You didn't invite me to Steeple Cross."

He *had* said it aloud. That is, he'd meant to say it, of course, but not quite so harshly. "I beg your pardon. I didn't mean..."

Except he had meant it, every word.

"I, ah... it seems I've made a rather drastic mistake." She pressed her palm to her forehead with a little laugh. "Goodness, what a muddle. But perhaps you'd be kind enough to allow me to explain my reason for coming?"

There *was* a reason, then. "Very well."

"Thank you. Have you heard from Lord Melrose since you left London, my lord?"

Ah, so she'd come here in search of Melrose, had she? But of course, she had. It made perfect sense. "It pains me to disappoint you, Miss Templeton, but I haven't seen Lord Melrose since the night you and your sister and Lady Fosberry fled Covent Garden Theater, and he chased after you."

Damn it, why had he brought *that* up? He didn't want to think about that night. He'd done his best *not* to think about it since he'd arrived in Oxfordshire, and had sworn to himself he wouldn't spare it any more of his attention.

Now here it was again, dragged right back into the present as surely as Juliet Templeton herself was. He could hear the whispers even now, as clearly as if he were still sitting in Melrose's box, the snickers and hisses, and her name on every pair of lips.

But this time, it was worse. This time, the memories were assaulting him in his own home. *She* was in his home, in his study, his sanctuary, where everything was in perfect order, just the way he preferred it.

No carriage accidents. No scandalous young ladies falling through the air into his arms, then dripping mud all over his spotless marble floors. No surprises.

But it was his sanctuary no more. Now he was destined to be cursed with the memory of her face every time he dared to lounge in front of his own fireplace.

"Lord Melrose wasn't chasing *me*, Lord Cross, but my sister, Emmeline."

"Indeed?" He'd heard otherwise.

Melrose had kissed one or other of the Templeton sisters, had embroiled one or the other of them in a scandal, then had fallen in love with... one or the other of them, and every wagging tongue in London insisted it was Juliet Templeton.

The wagging tongues seldom had the right of it, of course, but in this case, the rumors made sense. Why would Juliet Templeton want him, if she thought she could have Melrose?

"Of course. It was always Emmeline from the very beginning, Lord Cross."

"Forgive me, Miss Templeton, but Melrose didn't seem to be at all sure which sister he was chasing when he left the theater that night."

"That's curious, because he didn't appear at all confused when he came to Lady Fosberry's house that night and begged for my sister Emmeline's hand in marriage."

Melrose had made Emmeline Templeton an offer? *Emmeline*. Not Juliet, but *Emmeline*.

His heart gave a wild leap, but in the next breath he'd snatched the foolish organ up in his fist and squeezed until it dropped back into the center of his chest with a feeble whimper.

Good. That was where it belonged. Hadn't he learned anything this season?

"Your sister and Melrose are betrothed, then?"

"No. She refused him."

"*Refused* him?" Refused *Melrose*, the Nonesuch. Emmeline Templeton, a lady of no fortune and questionable reputation, had *refused* him? "Whatever possessed her to do something so foolish?"

"It's not foolishness, Lord Cross. There are a great many ugly rumors about my sister and me floating about London at the moment. If you'd remained in London another day, I daresay you'd have heard them yourself."

He'd heard them anyway. "Oxfordshire might be remote, Miss Templeton, but it is still in *England*."

"Yes, thank you, Lord Cross, I am aware of that. If you've heard the rumors, then you know the *ton* believes I'm the lady who, ah, caught Lord Melrose's attention."

"That's one way of putting it." Another, less charitable way was that Juliet Templeton had set her sights on Melrose from the first, and that everything she'd done during the season, including her flirtation with Miles, had been in service of her goal of marrying Melrose.

Some even claimed the Templeton sisters had made a wager with Lady Fosberry over whether or not Juliet would catch her quarry in the parson's mousetrap. Others—some of his guests among them —swore Melrose had made an offer to Juliet Templeton.

"One way, yes, but a lie, all the same. The trouble is, my sister is reluctant to expose me to the vitriol of the *ton*. She's refused Lord Melrose because she believes the only way to save me from ruin is for Lord Melrose to marry *me*, rather than her."

"That's absurd." Emmeline Templeton must be as mad as her sister was.

She shrugged, but her expression was troubled. "Emmeline insists the truth doesn't matter as much as what the *ton* believes to be true."

"She's not entirely wrong." Most rumors became so twisted and distorted as they passed from lips to ears, they ceased to bear any resemblance to the truth, but that never stopped anyone from believing them.

Or repeating them, whether they believed them or not.

"Of course, she's wrong. I disagree with her most vehemently, and have told her nothing the *ton* says could induce me to marry Lord Melrose in her place, but as far as I know, Emmeline is persisting in her stubborn refusals."

For God's sake. If it had been any other family, he wouldn't have believed a word of this, but the Templeton sisters had a gift for ridiculousness. "I don't know what any of this has to do with me, or why it should have induced you to come to Steeple Cross."

"Why, I want you to help me to dispel the worst of the rumors. They grow more outlandish and more hateful with every day that passes."

"It can't be so bad as you say—"

"Indeed, it is! If Emmeline hears the worst of it— and Buckinghamshire is also in *England*, my lord, so it's only a matter of time before she does—I'm afraid it will severely hinder Lord Melrose's and her chance at happiness."

It was all about her sister's happiness now, was it? Juliet Templeton was no fool. She knew how to play the best odds. If Melrose wanted Emmeline, then so be it. It didn't much matter which sister he married, as long as he and his massive fortune married one of them. "I still don't see why you need *me*, Miss Templeton. Surely, Lady Fosberry can—"

"No, she can't. I adore Lady Fosberry, but she's... well, she's been a trifle... Lady Fosberry would be the first to admit she's rather a gossip, herself. The *ton* won't credit her denials, but *you*, Lord Cross, a serious, respectable gentleman who never engages in gossip—"

"The reason I don't engage in gossip, Miss Templeton, is that I don't choose to become involved in other people's affairs."

She blinked. "Well, no, not generally speaking, but this time—"

"I don't choose to become involved this time, either. It won't do the least bit of good." His denying the rumors would only stir the cursed business up again. The gossip likely wasn't as awful as she made it out to be, and if it was, well... an adventuress must reap what she'd sown, mustn't she?

Or something like that. "If this was your only reason for coming to Steeple Cross, then there's no need for you to remain any longer."

Her face fell. "You can't mean... you're asking me to *leave*?"

"I am, indeed. Tomorrow morning, preferably."

And with those words, his reputation for coldness and arrogance was sealed in a single, disgraceful moment. He, who fancied himself a perfect gentleman, had just told a young lady he *didn't want her here*. That she wasn't welcome in his home. She was his *guest*, for God's sake, for she'd become so as soon as she walked through his door, whether he'd invited her or not—and a guest who'd just been through a frightening ordeal, no less.

Well, then. It seemed he *couldn't* be trusted not to behave like an utter savage, after all. Barnaby was going to be furious when he found out.

"But surely you must see that my leaving Steeple Cross will appear to be a confirmation of the rumors! The quickest way to put them to rest is for the *ton* to think you invited me, and that we're friends."

"*Friends*?" With very few exceptions, he didn't *have* friends. Certainly not any who were young ladies. They all thought him condescending, bad-tempered, and far too serious for a man of his years, and the devil of it was, they were *right*. He was all of those things, just as his father before him had been. He hadn't any patience for silly young ladies, and even less for witless gentlemen.

37

In truth, he had little patience for anyone.

If he'd been fool enough to think Juliet Templeton was any different than any other young lady in London, then he'd certainly paid the price for his folly. He'd continue to pay it, too, for as long as she remained at Steeple Cross. "My decision is final, Miss Templeton."

"But... I don't understand. *Aren't* we friends, Lord Cross? Was I mistaken?"

Something tugged at him then, like a hook in his chest, but he ripped it out and flung it aside before it could tear a hole in his flesh, or sink its pointed tip into any major organs, like a lung, or a kidney.

Or worse, his heart.

If the season had taught him nothing else, it proved he *did* have one, after all, and it was as disruptive a thing as he'd always feared it would be. "We were never friends, Miss Templeton, merely passing acquaintances. If that."

"I see. Well then, I suppose there's nothing more to say. I won't trouble you again, Lord Cross."

She left the study without looking at him again, and that was the end of it. He was rid of Juliet Templeton, and with far less fuss than he'd thought possible. He dropped into his chair, but instead of the gratitude he should have felt, he couldn't stop thinking of the way she'd felt in his arms tonight.

He'd never held her before, had hardly laid a finger on her when they'd been together in London, other than to take her arm. But he'd thought about touching her dozens of times. He'd even gone so far as to imagine how she'd fit against him—if her head would rest over his heart, and if her lips could reach the hollow of his throat if she rose to her tiptoes.

It had taken a scandal for him to come to his senses, and realize she didn't belong there.

She hadn't then, and she didn't now.

The sooner Juliet Templeton was gone from Steeple Cross, the sooner he could forget she'd ever been here at all.

CHAPTER
FOUR

That night, Juliet was tormented with frightful nightmares, which was quite a feat, considering she never once shut her eyes after the housemaid closed the bedchamber door behind her.

These were waking nightmares—nightmares where she risked life, limb, and the last shreds of her sanity to attend a house party she hadn't *even been invited to*, given by a man she now suspected had fled London specifically to escape her.

She desperately needed a word with Lady Fosberry, but she couldn't quite bring herself to disturb her ladyship's sleep after their dreadful ordeal. So, there was little for her to do from dusk to dawn aside from stare at the ceiling and try to determine how she could have ignored every sign warning her to stay far away from Steeple Cross.

If she hadn't believed in portents and ill omens before this ill-fated trip to Oxfordshire, she did *now*. She'd done something to earn the wrath of the universe, and it must have been very wicked, indeed, because as dreadful as these past few years had been,

41

none of it had given her as much pain as that scene in Lord Cross's study last night.

When he'd appeared out of the darkness just when she was most desperate for him, like a guardian angel, or some sort of romantic hero, there'd been a fleeting moment when she'd been certain that he... that they...

Well, it didn't matter now, did it?

She'd been wrong, and it was just that sort of silly, starry-eyed foolishness that had led her into this predicament in the first place. If she could flee Steeple Cross without laying eyes on Lord Cross again, she'd climb out the window right now, and never venture as much as a toe into Oxfordshire ever again.

But she couldn't vanish without a word to Lady Fosberry, and she didn't have a carriage at her disposal, in any case. There was nothing for it but to wait for Lady Fosberry to wake, and consult with her about what was best to be done.

So, she waited, the minutes crawling by with the same maddening sluggishness as the long winters at home in Herefordshire, until she could stand it no longer, threw the coverlet off and slipped through the connecting door between their bedchambers. "Lady Fosberry? Are you awake?"

"Mmmphh," said the blanket-covered lump in the middle of the bed.

"My lady? I beg your pardon for disturbing you, but a difficulty has arisen."

"Mmmphh."

Juliet crept closer, and nudged at the lump's shoulder. "It's Lord Cross, my lady."

"Mmmphh?"

"Yes." Juliet leaned closer to the lump, raising her

voice. "He's, ah... he's asked me to leave Steeple Cross at once."

"Mmmphh!"

"It seems I wasn't invited to attend the house party after all, and—oh!" Juliet leapt backwards as Lady Fosberry bolted upright with such violence a silk cushion flew off the bed and tumbled onto the floor. "My goodness, my lady, you scared the life out of me!"

"Not invited! Why, what utter nonsense! I was invited, and you came as my guest!"

"Yes, but Lord Cross says *he* didn't invite me, and he..." Juliet swallowed. "He doesn't want me here."

"Not want you? Not want *you*! Open the draperies this instant, Juliet."

Juliet rushed to do as she was told, while Lady Fosberry snatched up a handful of pillows, pummeled them into submission, then thrust them against the headboard behind her. "Give the fire a poke as well, will you? Yes, there's a dear girl. Now, come sit here, and tell me all of it."

She *had* told Lady Fosberry all of it—being flung out of an earl's house wasn't a terribly complicated thing, after all—but one didn't argue with Lady Fosberry when she was in a fit of outrage. "Lord Cross informed me last night that he—"

"Last night! You mean to tell me that wicked man had the audacity to demand you leave Steeple Cross not an hour after you were *nearly killed* in a carriage accident?"

That was a bit of an exaggeration, but she wasn't in any mood to defend Lord Cross. "Yes, I'm afraid so."

"I can hardly believe my ears. I'm fond of Cross,

43

despite what people say about him. I've always believed he hid a tender heart under all that brusque-
ness, but perhaps I've been mistaken all along."

Juliet said nothing, and kept her gaze on the fold
of the coverlet she was worrying between her fingers,
but her heart was sinking.

"For pity's sake, what ails the man?" Lady Fosberry had grabbed one of the stray pillows, and was
squeezing the life out of it. "Why shouldn't he want
you here?"

"Because I'm a scandal."

"Nonsense, Juliet! You're not—"

"I *am*. My mother is a notorious adulteress, my
lady. The entire *ton* has washed their hands of the
Templetons, and that was *before* Emmeline's, er... *en-
tanglement* with Lord Melrose this season. Aside from
you, all of our old friends have long since abandoned
us. I should have known I wouldn't be welcome
here."

"My dear child, you're mistaken—"

"No, I'm not. There was no mistaking the horror
on Lady Cecil's face when she caught sight of me in
the entryway last night. She couldn't have been more
horrified if a dozen rats had scurried through the
door."

At the mention of Lady Cecil, Lady Fosberry's face
went darker than the thunderclouds outside the window. "Oh, I can well imagine Lady Cecil set upon you
like a spitting, hissing, rabid cat. But you mustn't let
her upset you, dearest. She's an ill-tempered,
haughty old harridan. If anyone shouldn't be here,
it's *she*."

"Lord Cross *invited* Lady Cecil and her nieces."

Lady Fosberry snorted. "Yes, well, I daresay he'll

regret that soon enough. I've seen him cross the entire length of a ballroom to avoid her."

"Lady Cecil won't be the only one here to turn up her nose at me, my lady." She hadn't expected all of Lord Cross's guests would welcome her with open arms, but neither had she realized there would be so many of them at Steeple Cross.

Weren't hunting boxes meant to be small, well... boxes? Lodges of some sort?

Steeple Cross was an elegant, turreted affair of handsome gray stone, with a great many windows and arches and peaked roofs and such things, with aristocrats crowded into every corner of the place. It was rather like being in London, only worse.

One could *leave* a London ballroom.

But a house party, somewhere deep in the Oxfordshire woods, trapped in a house with dozens of aristocrats, all of them eager to show their disapproval of her? That was a nightmare in the making, and one she should have foreseen, only...

Even if she had, she never would have imagined Lord Cross would be one of them.

She rose from the bed, wandered to the window and twitched a stray fold of the heavy silk draperies aside. The rain had sputtered to a dismal dribble, but the angry clouds above were swollen to bursting, threatening another deluge.

Of course, his hunting box must be *here*. It was so very *him*, to have chosen the least hospitable place in England to have his party, a place so enveloped in darkness that she may as well be trapped in the blackest bowels of—

"Are you quite certain about Lord Cross not wanting you here, dearest? The housemaid who attended me last night regaled me with quite a tale about how he vehemently defended you from an attack by Lady Cecil."

He had defended her, yes, and she'd been grateful to him for it, but that kindness had withered and died in the face of what had followed, because as awful as Lady Cecil had been, he'd been worse. "I'm certain."

"But he was so gallant last night! My dear, the way he whisked you right out of the air and into his arms was nothing short of miraculous." Lady Fosberry let out a girlish sigh. "Why, I've never seen anything like it before."

"He didn't have much choice. It was either catch me, or let me crash down on top of him. It was less an act of gallantry than one of self-preservation."

"Even so, not one man in a hundred could have managed such a feat. I shudder to think what might have happened to you if it hadn't been for Lord Cross."

"I don't deny it was impressive of him." The instant he'd closed his arms around her, the cold and wet had melted away as if they'd never been, and for those precious few, fleeting moments, she'd believed he was pleased to see her.

But his voice, when he'd welcomed her to Steeple Cross... perhaps she should have known what would happen, the moment she heard his voice.

Before last night, it had never made any sense to her why people persisted in describing his voice as cold. She'd never found it so. Oh, it might sting at times, but it put her in mind of rich morning chocolate that singed the tongue a bit before it melted into a dark sweetness.

Last night, though, for the first time since she'd

met him, that sliver of ice in his voice had been meant for her alone. Underneath the smooth veneer of politeness, it had been cold and tight, like a clenched fist inside a smooth kid glove.

Harbinger of doom, indeed.

"Come here, dearest." Lady Fosberry beckoned to her.

Juliet abandoned her post by the window, and dropped onto the edge of the bed with a sigh. "Perhaps I should be thanking Lord Cross for banishing me. I daresay I wouldn't have enjoyed myself much." Now that he'd refused to help stem the flood of rumors, there was no reason for her to stay.

"Oh, dear. You *are* fretting, aren't you? Well, this isn't the first time Lord Cross has put a frown on a young lady's face." Lady Fosberry tapped the space between Juliet's brows with her finger. "Such a pretty face, too, to be spoiled with a deep groove here."

"There, is that better?" Juliet dug up a smile from somewhere, and stretched it across her lips with an effort that made her teeth ache, but it must have appeared sincere, because Lady Fosberry gave her hand an affectionate pat.

"Much better, yes, but this is all quite puzzling, isn't it? Lord Cross has never suffered from an excess of charm, but for him to be so utterly lost to decency that he'd actually toss a young lady—"

Lady Fosberry broke off, eyes narrowing. She was quiet for a moment, tapping her chin, then she went on in an entirely different tone. "Indeed, it's *quite* unlike him. I've never known him to become so agitated over any young lady before. Tell me, dearest. What else did he say?"

"Nothing to any purpose."

He'd had quite a lot more to say, but she was weary of talking about Lord Cross, and weary of thinking about him. "I'll need a carriage. Do you suppose Lord Cross will lend us one of his? I could meet Fowler at The Fox, and return to London with him, and go on to Buckinghamshire from there."

"Hmm?" Lady Fosberry asked absently. "What's that, dearest?"

"A carriage, my lady, to take me away from Steeple Cross. I—"

"Take you away? Oh, but you can't leave, Juliet! It's out of the question."

Had Lady Fosberry not heard a word she'd been saying? "But I must. Lord Cross has insisted upon it."

"Oh, but you can't possibly go now. It's... it's raining!" Lady Fosberry waved a hand rather wildly at the window. "And... and you've been through a dreadful ordeal! You'll certainly be traumatized if you ride in a carriage again so soon."

"Traumatized? Why, not at all, my lady." It would be far more traumatic for her to remain in a place where she knew she wasn't welcome.

"But you... I—I can't possibly leave this morning, dearest! Why, I daresay I'll fall into hysterics if I venture onto the roads in this weather after coming so very close to death yesterday!"

"There's no need for you to accompany me, my lady. I can—"

"I won't send you off in a carriage alone, Juliet. No, indeed! I'm certain I'll be as fit as ever tomorrow morning. We'll discuss it again then, shall we?"

Tomorrow! That was a lifetime away. She could hardly bear to stay here another hour, much less twenty-four of them, but how could she refuse? Given their brush with death, a single day of rest didn't seem all that much to ask. "Yes, all right. I'll come check on you later."

"Thank you, dearest."

She went back through the door connecting her bedchamber to Lady Fosberry's, stopping in the middle of the room to eye the bed. How tempting it was, to simply crawl into it, pull the covers over her head, and remain there until tomorrow morning.

But no. She may be a scandal in the eyes of Lady Cecil and her ilk, but the truth was, she hadn't done anything wrong. Somehow, she kept losing sight of that.

She *hadn't done anything wrong*, no matter what Lord Cross thought of her, and she wouldn't cower under the covers in her bedchamber as if she had.

Instead, she marched to the door, pausing in front of the looking glass to tidy her hair, and smooth her skirts. A pale lady with violet smudges under her eyes stared back at her. She looked an utter fright, but she threw her shoulders back, and lifted her chin.

Until tomorrow, she was Lord Cross's guest, whether he wanted her here or not.

So, she'd go down to the breakfast parlor as any other guest would, find Lord Barnaby, and thank him properly for all the kindness he'd shown her and Lady Fosberry last night.

Then she'd come back upstairs, crawl into the bed, pull the covers over her head, and stay there until she could leave this place and the Earl of Cross behind her for good.

CHAPTER
FIVE

S teeple Cross was an appalling place. A ghastly, vile, dreadful place.

Juliet paused on the threshold of the breakfast parlor to scowl at the enormous, hand-carved walnut monstrosity that served as the dining table. It was polished to such a merciless gloss it reflected the blinding glare of the silver chafing dishes marching in an orderly fashion down the sideboard.

Every room, every window, and every stick of furniture at Steeple Cross was spotless, ruthlessly elegant, rigidly symmetrical, and so lifeless it was like a mausoleum piled high with corpses from which every drop of blood had been drained.

The library was the worst of it. She'd stolen a peek inside as she'd made her way to the breakfast parlor, and dear God, those poor books!

There were thousands of them, each one organized by subject, then grouped by categories within each subject, arranged in descending order by height, alphabetized by the author's surname, and placed onto acres of spotless mahogany shelving according to the shade of their leather bindings.

They'd been sorted, then sorted again, then cross-sorted a third time until she'd gone cross-eyed just looking at them. Perhaps she'd rearrange a few of them before she left Steeple Cross, so scientific inquiry overlapped with romantic novels, animal husbandry with religion, and the Latin translations with the Greek until a comfortable chaos reigned.

It was all so resoundingly the epitome of a wealthy gentleman's elegant country estate it might have been copied from a painting, right down to the collection of sweet-faced young ladies lingering over their morning chocolate, arrayed around the dining table like a collection of porcelain figurines.

Had they come with the house, perhaps?

A chuckle may have escaped her then—just a tiny, soft one, but every head swung in her direction, and one by one the sweet faces turned sour. A silence so frigid it might have frozen the tea fell over the room, until at last Lady Cecil's nieces rose from their places and, with airs of gravely offended virtue, swept from the room. Lord and Lady Kimble's daughters followed, their cheeks coloring, either with temper, or embarrassment.

Well, that was plain enough, wasn't it? Juliet's appetite fled in one sickening heave, but she slid into a chair and stared down at her own blurry reflection in the polished tabletop. Why had she come down here, and given them a chance to deal her such an ugly snub? Pure stubbornness, and no better reason—

"I shouldn't mind them, if I were you."

Juliet jerked her head up, and found one fair-haired young lady had remained at the table, a pretty teacup with a delicate pink rose pattern balanced between her dainty fingers. "I beg your pardon?"

The lady nodded at the door. "They weren't terribly good company, anyway." She took a calm sip of her tea, and offered Juliet a friendly smile. "Good morning."

"Er... good morning."

"It doesn't look as if there will be much hunting today, does it?" The young lady glanced out the window, frowning at the dark clouds scudding across the pale gray sky.

"No, I expect not." Though Lady Cecil's nieces had done an admirable job maiming their prey this morning, hadn't they?

"I'm Lady Cora Drummond. Have you just arrived at Steeple Cross?"

"Yes." Arrived just in time to leave again. "I'm Juliet Templeton. How do you do?"

There'd be a gasp now, or perhaps a little cry of dismay, or a squeak of outrage once Lady Cora Drummond connected her name to the recent scandal.

"Did you say *Juliet Templeton*?"

Oh, no. Perhaps she shouldn't have offered her name so readily. Was it too late to give a different one? "I—"

"The very same Juliet Templeton who's set every tongue in London wagging? My goodness, you're one of those matchmaking sisters, aren't you?"

Juliet hid her grimace by taking a gulp of her tea, then had to bite off a curse as the hot liquid burned her tongue. "Er, well..."

"All of London is talking about you," Lady Cora went on breathlessly.

They were doing a great deal more than talking.

They were gossiping, speculating, snickering, and cursing the Templeton name. "Yes, well—"

"I've *so* wanted to make your acquaintance!"

"You wanted to make *my* acquaintance?" Lady Cora must have mistaken her for someone else.

"Oh, yes! You and your sister are the only two people in London with any sense!" Lady Cora glanced at the door, and lowered her voice. "The *ton* is perfectly dreadful, isn't it? I was meant to come out this season, but my grandfather's passing prevented it. I was overjoyed at it—that is, not at my grandfather's death, of course—but to escape the season."

"The season *is* very—"

"Your matchmaking ideas are terribly clever! There must be something to your theories, too, because your sister is rumored to be marrying *Lord Melrose*." Lady Cora whispered Lord Melrose's name as if he were too glorious to be spoken of in anything but a reverent hush.

No, there'd been no mistake. Lady Cora knew exactly who she was.

"He's the Nonesuch. The *Nonesuch*, Miss Templeton. The gossips are claiming your sister bewitched him."

God in heaven, was that what people in London were saying now? That Emmeline had *bewitched* Lord Melrose? It sounded positively Machiavellian.

She jerked her hands under the table to hide their sudden, infuriated shaking. It was yet another wild rumor, and now that Lord Cross had refused to help stem the tide of gossip, there was no telling when the *ton* would weary of their rabid speculation.

What sort of man refused to help his own friends? If one couldn't rely on one's friends to defend them, who could one rely upon? But then Lord Cross had never been *her* friend, had he? He'd made that clear enough last night.

"... sister stole him directly out from under Lady Christine Dingley's nose, didn't she? And Lady Christine was this season's belle, too!"

"I wouldn't say she *stole* him." If Lady Cora insisted on tossing that word about, it would only be a matter of time before thievery was added to the list of the Templeton's sins.

"But every lady in London had her eye on Lord Melrose, and he fell madly in love with *your sister*!" Lady Cora clapped her hands together in delight. "Isn't it wonderful? I *do* adore a love story. How lucky you happen to be at Steeple Cross!"

It hadn't been lucky so far, unless one considered a carriage accident, a near-drowning, and humiliation at the hands of Lord Cross lucky.

Lady Cora cast an anxious glance around them, then reached across the table and grasped Juliet's hand. "You'll help me, won't you?"

"Help you? I don't see how—"

"My mother has taken it upon herself to arrange a match for me, and you'll never guess who she favors. Lord Montrose, Miss Templeton! Lord Montrose, of all people! I was so appalled when she told me, I couldn't say a single word."

"Oh, dear." Perhaps the less said about Lord Montrose, the better.

"You see my predicament, then. I must marry *someone*, I suppose. I know very well which gentlemen I *don't* want to marry, but I haven't the faintest idea which gentleman I *do*." Lady Cora clasped her hands under her chin, her eyes pleading. "You'll advise me, won't you?"

"Advise you?" Oh, no. Lady Cora couldn't mean—

"Advise me whom to marry, of course!"

Juliet stared at her, too horrified to say a word. Oh, *why* hadn't she paid more attention to the bad omens? The moment the rain started she should have insisted she and Lady Fosberry return to London at once. But no, she'd been too arrogant to pay heed to the warnings, and look at where it had landed her! "But Lady Cora, I can't possibly advise you on something so important as that!"

Lady Cora's forehead puckered. "Whyever not?"

"Because I could inadvertently choose the wrong gentleman, and doom you to a lifetime of misery!"

"Oh, I don't mean you can tell me whom to marry, of course, but you can employ your... your..." Lady Cora waved a hand around as she groped for a phrase. "Your magical matchmaking formula for my benefit."

Magical matchmaking formula? Oh, dear *God*. "There's no magic to it, Lady Cora. It's mere guesswork, with a bit of mathematical calculation thrown in. There's no formula, I assure you. It's little more than a game. You can't entrust your future to a *game!*"

"I don't see why not. The marriage mart is a game, as well. The only difference between them is that *your* game was clever enough to land your sister Lord Melrose."

What it had done was land them right in the middle of another scandal, one which could yet end in disaster. But how could she explain that to Lady Cora? The two of them might be of an age, but Lady Cora appeared to be as sweet, naïve, and innocent as ladies of a certain class were meant to be, whereas *she*...

Was older. Not in age, but in inexperience. Years older. Decades, really—

But wait. She didn't have to explain anything at all, did she? She was leaving Steeple Cross. "I'm afraid I can't help you, my lady. I'm leaving Steeple Cross tomorrow morning. I'm sure you understand a single day isn't nearly enough time to... to unleash the, er, the wonders of my magical matchmaking formula."

"Leaving?" Lady Cora's face fell. "But you can't *leave*, Miss Templeton!"

Before she could reply, steps sounded in the hallway outside the breakfast room, and a moment later Lord Barnaby entered. "Good morning, ladies. Coffee, if you please, Rowell." He strode toward the sideboard, piled a plate high with eggs, sausages, and honey cakes, then joined them at the table. "I trust you've recovered from your ordeal last night, Miss Templeton?"

"Thank you, yes." From last night's ordeal, that is. There seemed to always be another one lurking around the corner.

"Ordeal?" Lady Cora asked. "My goodness, what happened?"

Lord Barnaby turned to Lady Cora, and froze with his fork partway to his mouth. "Cora? Is that you? I'll be damn—"

"Lord Barnaby!" Lady Cora glared at him, scandalized. "I'll thank you to mind your language!"

"I beg your pardon, ladies." Lord Barnaby lowered his fork to his plate, his gaze lingering on Lady Cora's face with blatant admiration. "Why, Cora, how you've changed! I wouldn't have known you."

"It's *Lady* Cora, Lord Barnaby." Lady Cora's pink rosebud lips pinched into a disapproving frown. "For a gentleman who hardly knows me, your address to me is much too familiar."

"But we're old friends, aren't we?" Lord Barnaby gave her a charming grin.

"Not so old as that, and not so friendly, either." Lady Cora sniffed. "Still, I would have known *you* anywhere, my lord."

Lord Barnaby, who looked as if he relished Lady Cora's scolding, gazed at her with his chin in his hand. "Would you, indeed? I'm flattered."

"You needn't be. Everyone in London knows you by your wicked reputation."

"You wound me, Lady Cora." Lord Barnaby pressed a hand to his chest, his eyes dancing. "I'm not so very wicked, am I?"

"Wicked enough. Weren't you sent down from Oxford for playing cricket in Christ Church Chapel?"

"That? It was just a bit of youthful high spirits, Lady Cora, and anyway, it was years ago."

"*Two* years ago, I believe. And didn't you shoot Lord Lewellyn in the foot in a duel this past spring?"

"It wasn't his entire foot, merely his big toe."

"Then there was that disgraceful business at Lord Buckley's rout, with Lady Irving's pet pig and a pot of treacle—"

"Pardon me, Lord Barnaby, Lady Cora, but I must go upstairs and check on Lady Fosberry." Juliet scrambled from her seat and darted to the door. "I do hope you'll both enjoy the hunting party."

"Must you go, truly?" Lady Cora's pink lips turned down, her blue eyes shone as if they were a breath away from filling with lovely, crystalline tears, and she was looking at Juliet like a castaway watches a ship vanishing into the horizon.

"I—I'm afraid so." Oh, *why* must she disappoint the only young lady who'd shown her any kindness since the season's debacle? She might even have found a new friend in Lady Cora, and God knew she had few enough of those.

But *nothing* could induce her to stay here after what had passed between her and Lord Cross last night. He might sink to his knees and plead with her to remain at Steeple Cross...

Well, that was just another silly, romantic notion, wasn't it?

There was no need for her to imagine what she'd say to Lord Cross if he begged her to stay, because that was never going to happen.

CHAPTER
SIX

"I've made my decision, Cross." Barnaby threw himself into the chair across from Miles's desk, one leg dangling over his knee. "My fate is sealed, my destiny determined, my hopes and dreams at last revealed in all their exquisite glory."

"Oh? What's your destiny this time?" Miles didn't bother looking up from the papers scattered across his desk. Barnaby was forever discovering his destiny, and Miles did have a great many letters to write.

"Why, Lady Cora Drummond, of course. I've just seen her in the breakfast parlor. I'm going to marry her."

Miles's quill faltered, and he gaped over the edge of his spectacles at his cousin. "You haven't laid eyes on Lady Cora in years, Barnaby! How in God's name can you have chosen her as your viscountess already? You couldn't have spent more than half an hour with her at breakfast!"

"Half an hour is more than enough time to fall in love, Cross."

"It's not yet ten o'clock in the morning! No one

falls in love before ten o'clock in the morning." It was unseemly. "Love is no place for excess, Barnaby."

Barnaby gave him a pitying look. "Oh, Cross. You poor devil. You don't know a damned thing about love."

"I know a man should choose a wife with a bit more consideration than he does his morning pastry. You haven't even met all the other young ladies yet!"

"I don't need to meet them. My mind is made up. Do you approve of my choice?"

How could anyone *not* approve of Lady Cora? Indeed, it was she, more than any of the other young ladies he'd brought to Steeple Cross, who was ideally suited to become Barnaby's bride. She was intelligent, charming, and sweet-tempered, but not without spirit, for all her gentleness. "I do indeed."

A young lady like Lady Cora Drummond could be the making of Barnaby.

"Good man, Cross! There's only one small problem. She didn't appear to share my enthusiasm at breakfast this morning."

"Share your enthusiasm?"

Barnaby grinned with unmistakable relish. "She *despises* me."

"She doesn't despise you, Barnaby." Lady Cora wasn't the sort to despise anyone, and despite his occasional pets and freakish whims, no one despised Barnaby. Even *he* didn't despise his cousin, and he despised nearly everyone.

"Certainly, she does. Any lady of any sense would. I don't wish to shock you, Cross, but my reputation isn't quite as spotless as a prudent young lady might wish."

Nor a very *imprudent* young lady, if the truth were

told. "It may take a bit of coaxing to bring her around, but I'm certain you can win her over. I'll do whatever I can to advance your cause."

"That's good of you, Cross, but she doesn't seem overly fond of *you*, either."

No, people generally weren't. "How have I offended Lady Cora?" An unfriendly look or frown, a stray comment he might have better kept to himself? He hadn't the vaguest idea, but it was usually one of those.

"Never mind, Cross, it doesn't matter." Barnaby waved a dismissive hand. "As it happens, we have another resource at our disposal."

"We do? What sort of resource?" Not the gold waistcoat, he hoped.

"Why, Juliet Templeton, of course. You'll have to beg her pardon first for whatever monstrous thing you did to chase her away, and then persuade her not to leave Steeple Cross, but I have the utmost confidence in you, cousin."

"Juliet Templeton!" Miles tore off his spectacles and tossed them on top of the stack of letters on his desk. Would that name never cease to haunt him? "What has she got to do with it, and why in the world should I beg her pardon?"

If anyone should beg anyone's pardon, *she* should beg *his*. She'd descended on his house uninvited, like a swarm of locusts—or, well, *one* locust, but even one was too many—and now, predictably, she was throwing everything into disarray.

"Because of your abominable behavior, of course. You've frightened her off."

Frightened Juliet Templeton? Laughable. He'd never seen a lady less apt to be frightened of anything than she. "What makes you think she's going any-where?" She was, of course, going somewhere—*any-where* but here—but how did Barnaby know of it? Had she complained of him during breakfast?

"Oh, she's going. She told Lady Cora she was leaving tomorrow morning."

Well, that *was* good news. Just what he'd hoped for, in fact. She was nothing but a distraction. The sooner he was rid of her, the better.

He shot to his feet, suddenly too agitated to sit still another moment.

He *hadn't* acquitted himself last night quite as the gentleman he claimed to be, but it wasn't as if he re-gretted his harsh words to her.

Still, that shadow of reproach in her eyes—

"Stop that infernal pacing, will you, Cross? I haven't even told you the whole of it yet."

"What's the whole of it, then?" What could be worse than asking Juliet Templeton to remain at Steeple Cross when he'd nearly tossed her out his door last night?

"Well, you see, I was eavesdropping on Miss Tem-pleton and Lady Cora before I entered the breakfast room, and I heard Lady Cora ask—"

"Eavesdropping! For God's sake, Barnaby."

"... and I heard Lady Cora ask Miss Templeton to advise her on a choice of husband."

Miles froze mid-step. "Why the devil would Lady Cora want Miss Templeton to advise..."

Damnation. It was that infernal matchmaking nonsense again. All of London was buzzing about the Templeton sisters' matchmaking abilities, since quiet Emmeline Templeton had caught Mel-rose's eye. Lady Cora must have heard about it, and now she wanted Juliet Templeton to match-make for *her*.

And that... *that* was worse than anything.

"Miss Templeton must stay and help me win over Lady Cora. What have you got against Miss Templeton anyway, Cross? I think she's lovely."

Lovely, yes. Far too lovely for his peace of mind.

"If you beg her pardon, I daresay she'll agree to help. You did save her life last night, after all. That was a neat trick, Cross, plucking her out of the air as you did. How did you manage it?"

"Pure, foolish luck." With the emphasis on *foolish*.

"But for you, Miss Templeton might have broken a limb."

"Or her neck. What did she think she was *doing*, frolicking atop a carriage that was about to topple over the side of a cliff?"

Barnaby blinked at him. "*Frolicking*? It looked more like she was clinging for dear life to me."

"Well, what was she doing up there at all? What possible reason could there be for her to climb into the driver's box?"

"Lady Fosberry said she was attempting to retrieve a pistol from—"

"I'll tell you why she did it, Barnaby. Because Juliet Templeton can't stir a single step without it ending in theatrics."

She couldn't simply *walk* into a room. Oh, no, nothing so dull as that. She glided, or swept, or floated. On one memorable occasion, he'd even seen her gambol. Other ladies might sit in a chair, but she dropped into it like a plump, ripe bit of fruit from an overladen tree, or collapsed with graceful abandon. Her smiles were sunrises, her laughs a concerto, her voice silver bells drifting through the clear, cold air on a Christmas morning.

He'd never met a more aggravating lady in his life.

"Now, Cross. I don't think you're being quite fair to Miss—"

"Of *course*, she somehow contrived to drop from mid-air right into the cradle of my arms, as if fate gave her a shove when I was the only person in the entire world in a position to catch her!"

Fortunately, he didn't believe in fate.

But he did believe in chaos, and that was what Juliet Templeton was. "That woman is pure pandemonium, Barnaby, hidden behind a lovely face and eyes so innocent, so guileless, one would never guess what utter havoc lurks in those deep blue depths!"

Barnaby was staring at him. "Surely, that's an exaggeration—"

"Not a bit of it, Barnaby! As long as Juliet Templeton remains in this house, I foresee a fortnight of utter mayhem."

"Perhaps you'd better sit down, Cross, before you—"

"And I don't just mean a few spilled drops of port or a few shattered dishes, cousin. If we make it to the end of a fortnight without a ruination, a duel, and without Steeple Cross's roof caving in, we may consider ourselves fortunate!"

"For God's sake, Cross, do you hear yourself, man? And you accuse Miss Templeton of theatrics!"

"She can't remain here, Barnaby. I won't have it."

All of his meticulous plans for the next fortnight —the elegant dinners, the bottles of fine liquor stacked to the ceiling of his cellars, the blazing fires in every bedchamber, and the curated collection of young ladies he'd chosen for Barnaby—were going the way of the carriage yesterday.

A slow slide toward the edge of a precipice.

"Now just a moment, Cross. You can't mean to say you're going to toss her out the door. Lady Fosberry will take offense, and rightly so. You invited Miss Templeton here—"

"I *didn't* invite her! I haven't the vaguest idea what she's doing here."

"But she *is* here, Cross, and it'll cause a dreadful fuss if you send her away." Barnaby paused, studying him from under lowered brows. "Is this about what happened between you and Miss Templeton this season?"

Miles froze, and it took every bit of restraint he had to keep his expression neutral, and his voice calm. "Gossip, nothing more."

"It's not gossip if it's true, Cross. Is it true?"

It wasn't true. It *wasn't*, no matter if it felt as though she were haunting him. "What, that I'm madly in love with Juliet Templeton? That she bewitched me, and I spent all season chasing her, only for her to slip through my fingers? What do you think, Barnaby? Have you ever known me to lose my head over some chit before?"

"No, but it was bound to happen, wasn't it? And Juliet Templeton is rather tempting."

God, his face felt stiff, and his stomach was roiling. "Not to *me*."

Barnaby considered him for a moment. "I don't believe you, Cross."

"Damn it, Barnaby. I told you, it's nothing but gossip. I hardly know the girl. I don't have a thing to do with Juliet Templeton, and I am *not* begging her pardon. I refuse."

The silence that fell between them in the wake of this outburst wasn't of the comfortable, soothing variety. It bulged and swelled and twisted until Barnaby threw his hands up in the air. "Very well, Cross. Then you've plunged a knife right into my heart for no reason whatsoever. Your only cousin, too. I hope you're happy."

"I'm never happy to have inconvenienced you, Barnaby." Miles dropped back into his chair, rubbing his hand over his eyes. It was only the first day of his house party, he was already exhausted, and it was all Juliet Templeton's fault. Drama trailed after her like a dog on a scent. "Not to worry, cousin. Miss Templeton isn't going anywhere."

Barnaby looked up at him, his eyes flaring with hope. "She isn't?"

"Alas, no. Fetch Mrs. Poole for me, will you?"

"Yes, of course." Barnaby shot to his feet and fled out the door of the study, trusting without question that Miles would set everything to rights again at once.

And he would, but the draught of pride he'd be obliged to swallow first might choke him.

"Lord Cross?" Mrs. Poole appeared in the doorway. "You sent for me?"

"Yes, Mrs. Poole. Would you be so good as to fetch Miss Templeton, and have her come downstairs to my study? I wish to have a word with her."

"I believe Miss Templeton is next door in the library, Lord Cross. I saw her go in there myself just a short while ago."

"Very good. Thank you, Mrs. Poole."

Miles waited for Mrs. Poole to leave, then rose from his chair and made his way down the hallway. The door to the library was partway open. Juliet was indeed inside, and she was... what on earth was she doing?

Her back was to him, and she hadn't heard him enter, so he remained quiet, and watched as she selected a book from one of the shelves, glanced briefly at the title, then crossed the room and slid it between two books on a different shelf.

She was disarranging his bookshelves!

Why, it was outrageous, and yet... how often had he longed to do the same thing when he was a boy? Tip books sideways, leave smears on the windows, muss the spotless floors, and set all of his father's rigid right angles askew?

"I don't think *Romeo and Juliet* belongs next to Galileo's *Sidereus Nuncius*, Miss Templeton."

She froze, her fingers wrapped around the spine of Copernicus's *De revolutionibus orbium coelestium*, which was no doubt destined to end up buried between *Richard III* and *Julius Caesar*.

"I don't see why not." She turned and gave him a careless shrug. "Shakespeare had a good deal to say about astronomy. Have you forgotten your *Romeo and Juliet*, my lord? '*The brightness of her cheek would shame those stars, As daylight doth a lamp; her eyes in heaven.*'"

Naturally, she had a relevant Shakespeare quote right at her fingertips. "I remember it. I also recall your telling me that play is a romance, not a tragedy."

A *romance*, of all ridiculous things. But then perhaps *everything* was a romance, when one was Juliet Templeton.

"It is a romance. But I don't wish to argue with

you, Lord Cross. Indeed, you need not trouble yourself with me any longer. I'm leaving Steeple Cross first thing tomorrow morning."

"You mean to drag poor Lady Fosberry into a carriage so soon after last night's debacle?" He leaned a shoulder against a bookcase. "That's rather selfish of you, Miss Templeton."

"I suppose it would be convenient for you to find me so. I'm sorry to disappoint you, my lord, but Lady Fosberry is free to remain at Steeple Cross for as long as she likes. You did invite *her*, after all."

"You can't mean you intend to go back to London *alone*?"

"Not London, unless Lady Fosberry chooses to leave tomorrow morning. If she'd rather remain, then I'll go to the Earl of Hawke's estate in Charlbury. My sister is governess there. I'll remain with her until Lady Fosberry is ready to return to London."

A sister in Charlbury? How convenient, but then Juliet Templeton seemed to live a charmed life. No doubt the woodland animals would have joined forces to rescue her and Lady Fosberry last night, if he and Barnaby hadn't appeared. "I'm afraid that's out of the question, Miss Templeton. I can't spare a carriage to take you to Charlbury."

She shrugged. "No matter. It's eight miles from here, my lord. I'll ride. Unless you can't spare a single horse, despite having stables the size of Hyde Park?"

"It's raining." He nodded at the rain-streaked window.

"Then I'll get wet. Now, if you'll excuse me—"

"Wait. I—I need your assistance with a, er... a task."

There went her eyes, wide, then wider still, and so very, damnably blue.

"A task," she repeated flatly. "*You* are asking *me* to assist you with a task."

"Yes. You see, Lord Barnaby is—"

"You, who told me just last night, and in no uncertain terms that you didn't want me in your house."

"Well, yes, but—"

"You, who accused me and my sister of manipulating your dear friend Melrose."

"I wouldn't say *accused*—"

"*You*, who refused to help dispel the rumors about me, even while Lord Melrose and my sister's very happiness may depend on it. You're asking me to assist you with a task. Do I understand you correctly, Lord Cross?"

Good Lord, one's pride did burn going down, didn't it? "Don't forget, I did save you from going over the side of the hill with the carriage."

"You most certainly did not. I'd already jumped before I even knew you were there. I saved *myself*."

"Well, I kept you from hitting the ground." There was no denying that, at least.

"I would have preferred a cracked skull to such a reluctant rescue. *Here*." She shoved the Copernicus into his hands, and with a haughty toss of her head, marched toward the door.

It was an exit fit for a duchess, nearly as dramatic as her arrival at Steeple Cross last night had been. It would have been impressive, indeed, but for one thing.

He had no intention of letting her go.

CHAPTER
SEVEN

J uliet had always wanted to sweep from a room in a fit of self-righteous pique, her head high, nose in the air, and with an expression of offended dignity upon her face.

At last, she had her chance.

She gathered a handful of her skirts in her fist—sadly, they lacked the long train necessary for a *truly* majestic exit, but one made do with what one had—and commenced with flouncing off in high dudgeon. "If you'll be so good as to excuse me, my lord, I must go and pack my things."

She brushed by him, intending to march out the door without a backward glance, but he moved in front of her, blocking her escape. "Just a moment, Miss Templeton. We're not finished."

Goodness, he was tall, and a trifle piratical, with that dark scowl. "On the contrary, my lord. I'm *quite* finished."

"Not yet. You haven't given me a chance to change your mind."

"Nor will I." Why should she? "If you recall, last

night you were so eager to be rid of me, you were a breath away from setting your hunting dogs on me."

His lips twitched, and goodness, they were full, and so... firm. Had she never before noticed how firm they were?

"Nonsense. If I'd set the dogs on you, you wouldn't be standing here right now. They never miss their mark."

Was he *laughing* at her? "You wanted me out, and you didn't take any pains to hide it. If it hadn't been for Lord Barnaby, I'd have found myself swimming from Steeple Cross back to Chipping Norton last night. You'll forgive me then, when I say I can't help you."

"Certainly, you could, if you chose to."

"Very well, then. I don't choose to." High-handed, arrogant man! He'd as good as bundled her out the door as if she were soiled linens last night, and now he had the gall to demand a favor from her? "You've made it clear we're not friends, Lord Cross. I don't owe you anything more than I would a stranger."

"Perhaps not, but the favor I require is for Lord Barnaby, not myself."

If he'd uttered almost any other name, she'd be halfway up the stairs by now, but while Lord Cross deserved to be left alone to ponder his sins, Lord Barnaby had been kind to her, and he'd taken such tender care of Lady Fosberry last night. "Oh, very well. What do you want?"

"Lord Barnaby has, er..." He ran a finger under his cravat, jerking the tightly wound cloth away from his throat. "He's, ah, fallen in love with Lady Cora Drummond."

"That's perfectly delightful, my lord. I wish them

both joy, but I fail to see what Lord Barnaby's affection for Lady Cora has to do with me."

He gave his cravat another tug, and cleared his throat. "Lady Cora hasn't fallen in love with *him*."

Oh. That was something of a dilemma. It explained why Lord Barnaby's flirtations had met with such a cold response from Lady Cora at breakfast this morning. "Then I'm sorry for him, but I don't know what I'm meant to do about it, unless Lord Barnaby wants me to court Lady Cora *for* him."

"That is, in a manner of speaking, precisely what he wants, Miss Templeton."

She snorted, but when Lord Cross merely raised an eyebrow, her laughter died on her lips. "What? But... *what*? That's ridiculous! A lady doesn't court another lady on behalf of a gentleman!"

"She does if she happens to be a matchmaking, er... genius?" Lord Cross's lips tightened, as if merely saying that last word had caused him physical pain.

"But I'm *not* a matchmaking genius! I don't know a blessed thing about matchmaking. I don't possess a gift for choosing matches, no matter what every gossip in London might say."

"Of course, you don't. The very notion is preposterous."

Surely, there wasn't any need for him to agree *quite* so vehemently. "Well, then?"

"It doesn't matter whether you're a matchmaking genius or not, Miss Templeton. What matters is Lady Cora *believes* you are. If you suggest to her that Lord Barnaby is a proper match for her, she'll listen to you."

"But she *shouldn't* listen to me." If she hadn't just been through a disastrous season of her own, she might have been naïve enough to believe she could help Lady Cora, but six weeks in London had taught her otherwise. "Suppose she did as I advised, and ended up miserable? Lord Barnaby seems a pleasant young gentleman, but I believe he's considered something of a rogue."

She wouldn't be the one to doom that sweet young lady to a lifetime with a libertine.

"Barnaby is high spirited, but he has an honest heart, and he's a gentleman. I believe his affections for Lady Cora to be both, er... ardent and genuine, if a trifle rash."

Rash? Lord Barnaby was the opposite of his cousin, then. "Even if I were to undertake such a mad scheme, I can't promise a favorable outcome, nor will I agree to suggest anything at all to Lady Cora that I don't believe is in her best interests."

"If I didn't believe Lady Cora and Barnaby would make each other happy—as happy as a marriage ever makes anyone, that is—I wouldn't be in favor of the betrothal, but they've been friends since they were children. They're an ideal match."

Was there even such a thing? She'd thought so, once, but if anything could knock romantic notions from a young lady's head, it was the London marriage mart.

Still, it *was* dreadfully tempting to see if she could manage the thing, but Lady Cora and Lord Barnaby weren't chess pieces to be manipulated at her whim. "I wish Lord Barnaby good luck with his courtship, Lord Cross, but I can't help you."

She tried to duck around him, but he caught her wrist to stop her. "Not even if I give you the very thing you want most?"

"How presumptuous you are, to think you know what I want." She glanced down at his hand. He wasn't wearing gloves, and there was an ink stain on his index finger, the single, tiny blot disturbing his otherwise flawless appearance.

She couldn't tear her gaze away from that blot—

"But I *do* know, Miss Templeton. You told me yourself." His gaze followed hers to their joined hands, and when he raised his eyes to meet hers again, his had darkened to a deep, moody black.

"Told you?" Dash it, her voice had gone all low and husky, and her lips had just parted in invitation —er, that is, her mouth had fallen open in shock. Yes, that was a much better explanation. "Just, ah... just what is it I want, my lord?"

"Have you forgotten so soon, Miss Templeton? Why, it was only last night you were begging for my assistance with—"

"*Begging*? I've never begged you for anything in my entire—"

"Begging for my assistance in this prickly business between Melrose and your sister. Something about Miss Emmeline refusing Melrose's suit on account of the scandal, I believe?"

"You mean to say if I agree to stay and assist you with your, er... matchmaking endeavors—" Dear God, even the words made her cringe— "you'll help dispel the worst of the rumors?"

"I'm proposing an exchange of favors, yes."

"How shameless you are, Lord Cross." She jerked free of his grasp. "To demand an exchange of favors for a service you should do out of the goodness of your heart, in order to help your friend, Lord Melrose."

He gave her a careless shrug. "I don't have a good heart, Miss Templeton. Ask anyone."

No heart? Was that how he saw himself? He'd acted a perfect beast since she'd arrived at Steeple Cross, yes, but she didn't doubt the goodness of his heart—

"As fate would have it, Miss Templeton, we're in a unique position to help each other."

Was it fate that had a hold on them, or a curse? Was there even a difference between the two, and if not, did it matter? Lord Cross was offering her what may well be a last chance to help Emmeline find happiness.

What choice did she have, but to take it?

Lord Melrose may yet persuade Emmeline to become his countess, regardless of the vicious gossip, but Emmeline had been adamant in her refusals when he'd offered for her in London. And surely one of her sisters would have written her by now, if there were any welcome news? The silence from that quarter was a bit worrying—

"Do we have an agreement, Miss Templeton? Lady Cora and Lord Barnaby in exchange for your sister and Melrose?"

He made it sound bloodless, indeed.

Yet it didn't have to be, did it? Her visit to Steeple Cross had been ill-conceived, ill-timed, and ill-executed, but if she truly *could* help bring Lord Barnaby and Lady Cora together, and see them happy in each other, mightn't it help restore her flagging faith in love? Perhaps she wasn't destined for a happy ending herself, but to give up on love entirely was unthinkable.

If one lost that faith—if *she* lost it—what did she have left?

"Well, Miss Templeton?"

He was gazing down at her, his handsome face half hidden in the shadows cast by the firelight. He looked a perfect devil, with those stern lips and dark, gleaming eyes.

If a lady was going to wager her soul, she'd best make it worth it, hadn't she? "Very well, my lord. We have an agreement, as long as you're willing to make one final concession. It's just a tiny, insignificant thing."

He let out a sigh so heavy it threatened to snuff out the fire. "What now?"

Oh, he wasn't going to like this at all, but then that's what made it so delicious. "I want you to say *please*."

Silence. Then, in a tone that could only be described as a growl, "You want me to *what*?"

She ran a fingertip over the marble mantel, fighting a smirk. "I want you to ask me once more for your favor, but this time, I want you to say *please*."

It was childish of her to take such delight in tormenting him, but the thrill of sweet vengeance was rushing through her veins. It wasn't every day such an arrogant, overbearing lord was forced to beg a scandalous lady for help, especially after he'd made it clear he could hardly stand the sight of her.

But if there was ever a man who needed a firm set-down, it was the Earl of Cross.

"Miss Templeton, will you *please* do me the honor of favoring me with your assistance with my cousin's courtship of Lady Cora Drummond?"

Were his teeth clenched? They were! Why, how tremendously gratifying. She bit her lip, but it was no use. She could feel the pull of a wicked little smile in her cheeks. "If I didn't know it to be impossible, Lord Cross, I might believe *you'd* just begged *me* for a favor."

"I *did*," he ground out. "Do we have an understanding?"

She gazed up at him, into the dark eyes she'd so admired in London. They were narrowed to slits, and his mouth was pulled into a forbidding line. He was, once again, the detached, imperious earl every young lady in London feared.

But *she'd* never feared him, and she didn't fear him now. "Will you promise to do as I say, without question, as regards the courtship? I may not be a matchmaking genius, but I imagine I know more about it than *you* do, and I refuse to argue every point with you."

"Yes," he muttered, his teeth still clenched. "I promise."

She raised her chin, and met that fearsome stare without a quiver. "Then I believe we have an agreement, Lord Cross."

CHAPTER EIGHT

Three days had passed since Miles had struck his bargain with Juliet Templeton. Three calm, quiet, peaceful days, days in which he hardly heard her voice, or saw her face.

There were no theatrics. None of his volumes of Shakespeare went astray, only to be discovered days later among his history tomes, or his father's political discourses. There wasn't a speck of mud on his entryway floors. There were no brawls, duels, ruinations, or conflagrations.

It had been, dare he say... serene?

Yet somehow, they'd been the longest three days of his life.

Juliet attended dinner every evening, but she spoke only to Lady Fosberry, Barnaby, and Lady Cora and her mother. If he did happen to come across her during the day, she was invariably gazing out a window, through the rain-streaked glass to the grounds beyond.

Alone. She was always alone, but if she was lonely, it wasn't for *his* company.

If their paths did happen to cross, she pretended not to see him.

Which was how he preferred it, of course. He didn't need Juliet Templeton hanging about, distracting and provoking him, her dark lashes fluttering over those deep blue eyes, a stream of nonsense issuing from between those parted red lips, the soft tendrils of her dark hair against the white skin of her neck making his fingertips ache to touch, to stroke...

Indeed, he was *grateful* for the reprieve, because while she may have gone dormant, like a caterpillar snug in its chrysalis, she was sure to find her way back out soon enough, and then there'd be beating wings, and all manner of flapping and fluttering about.

Still, three days. Three long, silent, dreary days.

But if time *had* seemed to slow to a crawl, it had nothing to do with *her*. It was the blasted weather that had him so out of sorts. He'd been coming to Steeple Cross since he was a child, and he couldn't recall a more miserable August than this one. The rain had been an unceasing, torrential downpour. He couldn't even go out to ride, as a large portion of the grounds were flooded.

There was only so long a man could be cooped up indoors without becoming a trifle irritable.

So, when his temper snapped on the morning of the third day, it wasn't because Juliet didn't appear at breakfast. Nor was it anything other than the interminable gray skies that made him stalk through the house on the hunt for her. And when he found her tucked into a window seat in the library, it was the incessant rain and howling wind that made him demand, in a tone that did no credit to him as a gentleman, "Where have you been?"

And there went the blue eyes, wide, and then wider still, those diabolical black lashes fluttering.

"I—"

"Have you forgotten we have an agreement? I said I'd help you silence the rumors plaguing you, and *you* promised you'd help me with the small matter of my cousin's future happiness. Does that sound at all familiar to you, Miss Templeton?"

She laid her book aside. "I haven't forgotten, my lord."

"Well, then? When did you intend to begin with your matchmaking schemes?"

"I've already begun. I've been watching Lord Barnaby and Lady Cora for the past few days, and I have the most brilliant idea."

Juliet Templeton with a brilliant idea was sure to lead to mayhem, but the butterfly had battered her way free of the chrysalis, and there'd be no stuffing her back inside now. He dropped into a chair across from the window seat. "Very well, then. Regale me with your brilliance, Miss Templeton."

She beamed at him. "Bowls!"

"Bowls. You mean lawn bowls? The game?"

"Yes, the game with the jack? You *have* heard of it, have you not?"

"Of course, I've heard of it, but bowls require a bowling green, and I believe the lawns are currently underwater." For God's sake, if the weather were fine enough for lawn bowls, they'd be hunting right now.

"Indeed, they are, but the ballroom is perfectly dry, my lord."

"The ballroom? Why should the ballroom matter,

unless... good Lord, Miss Templeton, you're not proposing we play bowls in my *ballroom*?"

"I don't see why not. It's a very large one, with plenty of space to toss the bowls about."

"Toss the—"

"But I'm not proposing a *game* of bowls, my lord."

"You're not?" Thankfully, she hadn't utterly lost her wits.

"No, indeed. If we're going to go to all the trouble of turning your ballroom into a bowling green, then we must make a tournament of it, with teams and matches and a judge—perhaps Lady Fosberry will take that part—and winners and runners-up, and oh! What shall we use for prizes, my lord?"

Prizes? She *had* lost her wits. "We're not playing at lawn bowls in my ballroom, Miss Templeton."

"Whyever not?"

She asked as if this were a perfectly logical question, and even had the nerve to look puzzled by his objections. "Because it's a *ballroom*."

"Well, are you having a ball in there *right this minute*?"

"No, but—"

"Your guests are restless, my lord. The gentlemen are bored with no sport to amuse them, and the ladies... well, they're much as you'd expect ladies to be, when they're surrounded by cross, snappish gentlemen." This last was said with a rather pointed look that made his cheeks heat.

"Yes, I'm aware of that, Miss Templeton, but—"

"Well, what do you intend to do about it?"

"*Do*? Not a thing." Every gentleman in the county of Oxfordshire was cross and snappish, and there wasn't a blessed thing he could do about any of *them*, either. "I can't control the weather, for God's sake."

"There *is* no weather in the ballroom, Lord Cross. That's rather the point."

"No. It's out of the question."

"On the contrary, Lord Cross, *nothing* is out of the question. You promised you'd do whatever I asked, without argument."

"As regards the courtship, yes! But this doesn't have anything to do with—"

"I beg your pardon, but it certainly does. If Lady Cora and Lord Barnaby spend more time together, it will lead to a great sense of intimacy between them. In the confusion of the game, they may even clasp hands, or—" She broke off, her cheeks coloring.

"Ah, but intimacy could be dangerous, Miss Templeton. Don't you agree?"

"I, ah... well, I suppose there's a chance... that is, perhaps..."

Good Lord, but she was tempting when she was flustered. "Yes?"

She huffed out a breath. "It's a game of bowls, Lord Cross. I'm not proposing we lock them in a bedchamber together."

"You shock me, Miss Templeton." Except it wasn't shock that made every inch of him rise to sudden, aching attention.

Another blush rushed into her cheeks. "We'll play in teams of fours, with two ladies and two gentlemen per team, with Lord Barnaby assigned to Lady Cora's team."

"You forget I haven't agreed yet."

"A gentleman doesn't go back on his word, Lord

Cross. You *do* consider yourself a gentleman, do you not?"

"Of course." Most of the time. "I—"

"Because if you do intend to go back on your word, then Lord Barnaby may continue his courtship on his own. It will prove a bit difficult, as Lady Cora has taken to spending every afternoon reading in her bedchamber for want of anything else to do."

"I never said I intended to go back on—"

"I daresay Lady Cora would be delighted with a game of bowls. You were right about her, my lord. She's lovely, and would make a wonderful viscountess for Lord Barnaby. It's a pity, really, but if you no longer care about your cousin's happiness—"

"*Enough.* Bowls, it is. You're an utter menace, Miss Templeton."

Only a moment ago he'd claimed to be a gentleman, and a gentleman didn't accuse a young lady of menacing, but instead of the anger he deserved, she threw her head back in a laugh that *wasn't* charming, and *didn't* tug a pulse of heat from his lower belly.

She didn't look much like a menace now in her prim, sprigged-muslin day dress of some indeterminate color between blue and purple, every fold of the skirt in a graceful puddle on the floor at her feet, with her dark hair in a neat coil at the back of her neck.

But she could send everything sliding into chaos with one snap of her pretty fingers. He'd seen her do it, five days ago, merely by walking through the front door.

"Lawn bowls, in my *ballroom*." He slumped against his chair, defeated. "What could possibly go wrong?"

~

As it happened, there was a perfectly logical reason why lawn bowls were played on a bowling green, and not in a ballroom.

The thundering, pounding, unholy commotion of multiple bowls rolling towards multiple jacks at once was deafening. Bowls were flying about, knocking into his finely-papered walls and dinging his scrupulously shined floors.

Mrs. Poole had unearthed a few long lengths of carpet to serve as makeshift greens, but no amount of padding could drown out the sound of young ladies and gentlemen tossing bowls about with abandon, and shrieking and groaning as they struck each other's bowls, or managed to get near the jack.

"Good fun, eh, Cross?"

That was the trouble. It *was* good fun.

He couldn't recall having such fun in... well, ever, really. Who, other than Juliet Templeton, would ever have thought of playing bowls in a ballroom? Or that one could get so much pleasure from tossing a ball about, trying to hit other balls? It was utter chaos, of course, but then laughter often went hand in hand with chaos.

Somehow, he'd forgotten that, or... had he ever known it at all?

After a short time, he gave up worrying over the damage to the floors of a ballroom he never used, or agonizing over the imagined recriminations of a father who'd died more than a decade ago. Instead, he simply enjoyed himself, until his father's outraged voice faded to silence in his head.

"Lady Cora's aim is dead on, isn't it?" Barnaby's

eyes were bright, and his face flushed with laughter. "Watch, Cross."

Lady Cora sent her bowl flying across the ballroom, letting out a squeal of delight as it nudged against the jack, then gripped Juliet's arm, jumping up and down.

"Did you see that, Cross? Very pretty, Lady Cora!" Barnaby rushed back over to the ladies and handed Juliet her ball. "Go on, Miss Templeton. It's your turn."

Juliet stood in the middle of the melee with long strands of her dark hair coming loose from its coil, cradling the bowl in the palm of her hand. She took a dainty step forward, and with a graceful swing of her arm, tossed her bowl onto the green with such force it hit Lord Ambrose's bowl with a crack, and sent it skittering out of bounds.

Lady Cora let out a shout of glee as Juliet's ball rolled slowly down the green as if the hand of God himself were guiding it, until it came to a stop so close to the jack, one couldn't slide a shilling between them.

"Well done, Miss Templeton!" Barnaby cried, bursting into enthusiastic applause. "I daresay both you and Lady Cora would be crack shots. Do either of you hunt?"

Juliet's reply was lost in the commotion, but she was beaming, her blue eyes alight with the fun of it, much as they had been that day in London, when he'd escorted her through Lady Hammond's rose gardens, and she'd teased him about *Romeo and Juliet* being a romance, instead of a tragedy.

Which was nonsense, of course.

But she'd been right about the bowls. A bit of exercise was just what was needed, particularly for his younger guests, who'd grown dull and listless from too much time indoors. Now everywhere he looked, there were flushed cheeks, and wide smiles.

Or nearly everywhere.

Lady Cecil and her nieces had declined to participate in any activity that included Juliet Templeton, and a dozen or so of his haughtier guests had followed suit. One by one, they'd all turned up their noses at her.

The rumors were as ugly, as vicious as Juliet had told him they were. He already knew that to be the case, as he'd made a few discreet inquiries into the matter, and had had a long discussion with Lady Fosberry, but no one who witnessed his guests' behavior today could possibly doubt it. They were as swollen with venom as a swarm of insects bloated with blood.

Yet for all their staring and muttering and glowering, Juliet's smile never dimmed. She chatted with Lady Fosberry, and laughed with Lady Cora and Barnaby, her lips curved with delight.

There wasn't a shred of guilt on that conscience. No lady who'd schemed and machinated as the *ton* insisted Juliet had done could smile with such a pure joy as that. It was like the sun bursting over the horizon, warming everything it touched.

She'd told him the truth from the start. She hadn't had anything to do with the scandal, but was merely a victim of vicious gossip, as so many others before her had been.

Had he ever truly believed otherwise? Or was he just a coward?

It was much safer to hate Juliet Templeton than it was to love her...

Because in the end, it didn't make any difference. She might be as blameless as a newborn babe, her heart as pure as a beam of moonlight, as pristine as a blanket of sparkling new snow, and it wouldn't change a thing.

That infectious smile was meant to be shared.

And that... *that* was the danger of Juliet Templeton.

Not just dangerous for him, but dangerous for *her*.

That smile made him wish for things he had no right to want—made him forget he was still his father's son. How long would she survive with a man like him, in a place like this, before that sunrise of a smile froze on her lips? How long before it disappeared entirely?

A year? Maybe two?

Juliet Templeton wasn't for him. If he'd forgotten who he was for a few short, delirious weeks in London—had wished for something more—he had only to be grateful he'd regained his senses before he made a dreadful mistake.

CHAPTER
NINE

J uliet was balanced on her tiptoes, reaching for a book on a shelf above her head when Lord Cross burst through the library door, then slammed it closed behind him again with an echoing thump. "Why aren't Barnaby and Lady Cora betrothed yet?"

She jumped, the book's spine slipped from her fingers, and would have hit her on the head if he hadn't darted forward and caught it just in time. "For pity's sake, Lord Cross, you must stop bursting upon me like that! I'm right here, so there's no need for you to..."

Shout.

She never got the last word past her lips, because when she turned to face him, he was much closer than she'd anticipated, with one long arm braced on the bookshelf above her, his fitted coat straining at his shoulders, and her tongue grew too thick to utter a sound.

He was somber today, in a gray coat over a black waistcoat with gleaming silver buttons. He looked rather like one of the storm clouds still looming in the sky—a bit overwhelming, perhaps, but striking, too

—all dark-edged, masculine beauty, and tightly-leashed power.

My goodness. So much starch and polish shouldn't flatter him so outrageously, but a lady couldn't help but wonder what he was hiding underneath those austere colors and severe tailoring.

Well, perhaps not a *lady*, but it made *her* wonder.

"Yes?" He leaned a little closer, his eyebrows arching over gleaming dark eyes. "Did you wish to say something, Miss Templeton?"

"Er... no." Not aloud, that is.

"If you'd be so good as to listen, then." He peered down his arrogant earl's nose at her. "Your match-making schemes aren't working, and I demand to know what you intend to do about it."

Oh, so they were *her* schemes now, were they? "I believe you mean *our* matchmaking schemes, my lord, and it's much too soon to judge whether they're working or not. Anyone can tell you six days isn't nearly enough time to see a proper scheme through to its conclusion."

"Barnaby assures me a single glance is enough to inspire a lifelong passion. If that's the case, then why hasn't Lady Cora fallen in love with him yet? We only have a fortnight!"

For goodness's sake. Who but an arrogant earl would expect a couple to fall in love to best suit him? "It *is* tedious of them not to accommodate your wishes, my lord, but while they may be a perfect match from a purely practical standpoint, that doesn't mean they're destined to fall in love."

"Well, why not? I don't see why it has to be such a dark mystery. Why can't Lady Cora just get on with it? Stubborn chit."

"Because love isn't *logical*, my lord. A lady doesn't fall in love because you stomp your feet, and demand it." And thank goodness for *that*.

"I did *not* stomp my feet, Miss Templeton."

Not yet, at any rate. "While I do wish I could give you a date and time as to when Lady Cora might succumb to Cupid's arrow, I'm afraid I can only guess at what might happen from here. I already told you, I don't have any true insight into what makes people fall in love."

He waved a hand at her. "Well, make a guess at it, then. We're running out of time."

"It did occur to me she may regard him as her friend only, not as a suitor, or as a gentleman she could ever fall in love with."

"What's to be done, then?"

"That's what I came here to find out." She took the book from him and held it up. "Who better than Shakespeare to elucidate the mysteries of love?"

"Good Lord. *Romeo and Juliet*, again?" He reached over her head, pulled another book from the shelf and thrust it into her hands. "Better consult *A Midsummer Night's Dream*. It ends in marriage, rather than poisonings and death."

"Have you forgotten your Shakespeare, Lord Cross? Romeo and Juliet *do* get married, in the fifth scene of Act Two."

"They get married, yes, but then Juliet drinks poison, Romeo follows suit, and then they both die."

"Juliet doesn't die from the poisoning. She stabs herself with her dagger."

"She still *dies*, doesn't she? It's not a happy ending, Miss Templeton."

Juliet caressed the gilt-edged pages of the beautiful book with her thumb. Perhaps he was right, and she was mad to consider *Romeo and Juliet* a romance, rather than a tragedy. All that death was a bit problematic, romantically speaking.

But the lines that delineated romance from tragedy, and love from loathing were blurry, indeed, just as all such lines were. Life was an untidy affair, with the various parts forever bleeding into each other. One was just as likely to find a hint of tragedy in romance as they were to find a hint of romance in tragedy.

It was dreadfully messy, really, but there it was.

"You look grave, Miss Templeton, with that furrowed brow. Can it be that *Romeo and Juliet* is not as illuminating as you hoped?"

"Not at all. I'm merely refreshing my memory as to how they fall in love." She flipped a few more pages, then paused to read. "Ah, yes. Romeo thinks himself in love with Rosalind, but then he sees Juliet at a masquerade ball, and falls in love with her, instead."

"That's *it*? Pardon my cynicism, but I thought we'd concluded love at first sight is utter nonsense."

"No, *you* said it was nonsense. I never agreed with you, and I'll thank you not to put words into my mouth."

He raised an eyebrow at her waspish tone. "Very well. May I hope Shakespeare offers some other illumination into the quandary?"

"Well, of course, he does." Shakespeare always offered illumination. She bent over the book, and read the words aloud.

Did my heart love till now? Forswear it, sight,
For I ne'er saw true beauty till this night.

. . .

NE'ER SAW true beauty till this night. Saw true beauty...

Romeo sees her.

Could it be as simple as that? Thousands of lines of poetry, pages upon pages of prose, endless brush strokes across endless canvases, actors portraying doomed lovers stomping across the stage in a passion, wailing and clutching their breasts, all in the name of love.

After centuries of turmoil, could it be an essential part of love was no more than being truly *seen* by another person?

She looked up from the page. "He sees her."

"Who, Barnaby? Of course, he *sees* Lady Cora. We all see her."

"Not Lord Barnaby. *Romeo.* He sees Juliet as she truly is, and she sees him as he truly is, even though he's wearing a mask in their first scene together. Perhaps it's not any more complex than that."

"Forgive me, but if all it took was Barnaby and Lady Cora *seeing* each other, they would have fallen in love at age five, and I assure you, they did *not*. Barnaby splashed her with mud, and ruined her favorite frock."

"That's rather a charming story, really. If you'd concentrate on the matter at hand, my lord, then perhaps they'll have the chance to tell it to their grandchildren one day. We need to find a way to make Lord Barnaby and Lady Cora *see* each other."

"In some more dramatic way than across the table at dinner, I assume?"

"People see each other across dining tables every

day, Lord Cross, and they don't all fall in love, do they? I mean they need to *truly* see each other." How could two people fall in love without looking into each other's eyes?

They *were* the window to the soul, after all.

"How do you propose we arrange that? Bind them together, facing each other?" He gave her a maddening smirk. "I daresay Barnaby wouldn't object, but that would be highly improper."

"If you're concerned with propriety, Lord Cross, perhaps you'd better stay out of other people's love affairs altogether."

"Would that I could have stayed out of *this* one," he muttered. "I only mean to inquire how you attempt to achieve this deeper intimacy between them. Nothing untoward will do. Lady Drummond is extremely protective of her daughter's reputation."

Lady Cora's reputation was a concern, certainly. If the thing were to be done, it would need to be done delicately. How, though? What reason could she possibly come up with for Lord Barnaby and Lady Cora to stare deeply into each other's eyes?

She drummed her fingers against the smooth pages of the book, working to shake loose an idea. Dancing was one way to encourage a greater intimacy between couples, but this would require long, quiet moments of uninterrupted gazing without distractions, preferably in a quiet setting. Some sort of game, perhaps, or—

"Oh! I have just the thing!" Goodness, she was better at this than she'd thought.

"Pray don't keep me in suspense, Miss Templeton."

There was that amused drawl she'd heard him

use so often in London, the one that set her teeth on edge, and made shivers dart up her spine. The drawl she'd never decided whether she adored, or despised.

Messy, indeed.

"I propose we play a game. There won't be any hunting today, as the weather is frightful still, and your guests will once again be at loose ends. What better way to entertain them than with a parlor game?"

"Do *you* find parlor games entertaining? I find them unbearably dull."

She sank her fingernails into her palms to smother a sharp retort, offered him a sweet smile, and rose to her feet. "Very well, my lord. I'll leave you to come up with your own idea, shall I?"

"Wait, Miss Templeton." He caught her wrist. "I, ah... I beg your pardon."

Her palm stung from the press of her fingernails, but the firm pressure of his fingers, his thumb against her pulse point overwhelmed every other sensation. Could he feel the way it throbbed against him? Was he aware he was stroking his thumb lazily over that frantic fluttering, stealing her breath before it had a chance to reach her lungs?

Her gaze met his, the air between them crackling.

She swallowed. "Do you promise not to interrupt me again?"

"I swear it. Tell me the rest of your idea, won't you?"

"Very well." She withdrew her hand from his warm grip, and resumed her place in the window seat. "When I was younger—oh, it must be five years ago now—my eldest sister Euphemia came up with a game to keep us amused during the long winter afternoons in Buckinghamshire. She was brilliant at coming up with ways to entertain us."

Dear Euphemia. How she missed her.

"What sort of game?"

"Just a simple sketching game. Euphemia would assign each of us a partner—I nearly always got Helena, who is a year younger than me, while poor Emmeline was left to manage Tilly, our youngest sister, who is, er... quite high-spirited."

He smiled. "A high-spirited Templeton? *Shocking*."

"Isn't it? Now, Euphemia would mark the time, and we'd take up our pencils and draw our partner's face. Whoever had the best likeness was given some small token or other—I don't remember what now, but I remember doing the drawing, and looking intently at Helena's face."

"That's quite clever."

"My sisters are all clever, my lord." They couldn't boast of wealth, property, or even respectability, but they did have *that*. "We'd all become dreadfully silly and make faces at each other and so forth, as young girls do, but if we altered the rules a bit, and presented it as a parlor game—"

"And assigned Barnaby and Lady Cora to be partners—"

"They'd be obliged to gaze at each other for a not inconsiderable length of time, in order to draw each other's faces in detail."

"Long enough for Lady Cora to fall in love with Barnaby?"

As to that, she couldn't say, but it was a curious question, coming from him. Perhaps he wasn't quite the cynic he pretended to be. "You don't believe in love at first sight, Lord Cross. Remember?"

"It's not first sight, Miss Templeton. But no, I don't believe in it. It's utter nonsense. Outside of plays, people don't fall in love on the strength of one glance."

"How can you know?" How could anyone know anything about the way another person fell in love? "Why should it be time alone that determines whether two people fall in love?"

He shrugged. "It makes sense, doesn't it?"

"But that's just it, my lord. Love *doesn't* make sense. Two people can become attracted to each other at a single glance, so why can't they fall in love the same way?"

"Fiercely, intensely attracted. Fascinated, even." He swallowed, the impeccable knot of his cravat bobbing. "But that's not love."

"Lord Barnaby would say it *is*."

"Are we to take Barnaby's word for it? What does he know about love?"

Had he moved closer? The space between them seemed to have narrowed. "Well, I-I imagine he knows quite a lot about how he fell in love with Lady Cora."

"But surely, it can't be as simple as that? There must be more to love than a consuming, passionate desire between two people."

Consuming, passionate desire? Goodness. "It's either terribly, terribly complicated, or terribly, terribly simple."

"Which do you say it is, Juliet?" He leaned closer, his hands on the window seat on either side of her, his fingers brushing her hips. "Have you taken your lessons on love from *Romeo and Juliet*?"

"N-no." He was so close she could see the shadow

of a beard on his cheeks. She wanted to touch it, feel the rasp of it under her fingertips. "I don't think there is such a thing as lessons on love. I think there are as many kinds of love as there are people, and that each person falls into it in their own way."

"Do you speak from experience?" His eyes held hers, so dark and deep, like a pool of water at night. "Have you ever fallen in love at first sight?"

She thought she had, once. "I-I believe in love at first sight, I'm just not certain if..."

"What?" His voice was so soft, barely above a whisper. "You're not certain of what, Juliet?"

Juliet. She sucked in a shaky breath at his rough murmur of her name on his lips. "I'm not certain if I believe in it for myself."

"No?" He slid his thumb under her chin, and tipped her face up to his. "Why not? Why should love not be for you?"

She caught her breath at the soft touch, at the sparks he left in his wake. "I-I don't know."

"Ah, but I do." His eyes were half-closed, sleepy under the weight of his impossibly thick, long lashes. "You, Juliet Templeton, more than any other lady I've ever known, are destined for love."

Dear God, he was so close, his breath a soft, hypnotic drift over her lips. "I... I am?"

"Yes. Because you already carry it inside you. It's part of who you are."

"It's part of all of us, my lord." She wrapped her fingers around his wrists, because it was terribly important, somehow, that he understand this. "You, Lady Cora, your cousin—all of us."

"My cousin?" He asked, reaching out to trace her lower lip with his thumb.

They parted under the caress, and his gaze dropped to them at once, his eyes as dark as midnight. "Yes, Lord... Lord Barnaby, my lord."

"Lord Barnaby. My *cousin*, Lord Barnaby. Lord Barnaby and Lady Cora."

He jerked his hand away from her face and backed away, and just like that, the heat that had built between them cooled, and the moment between them was gone, as quickly as a snap of the fingers, the stomp of a foot, the turn of a page.

There was nothing to do, then, but to ignore her heart's last dying flutters. "We'll introduce the game after tea?"

"That's acceptable, yes." He cleared his throat, tugged his waistcoat down, and twitched the cuffs of his shirt into perfect alignment with the edges of his coat sleeves. "Until then, Miss Templeton."

He was gone before she could answer, gone as quickly as the storm clouds rushing across the sky, leaving her alone in the window seat with Shakespeare and his star-crossed lovers, Romeo and Juliet.

CHAPTER
TEN

I f Miles had realized drawing Juliet's face would be like touching her, his pencil like his fingers stroking over her soft skin, he would have volunteered to be the timekeeper.

He'd already touched her today—her wrist, her pulse leaping under his fingertips, and the sweet swell of her lower lip, but those simple touches had jolted up his arm as if he'd been struck by lightning.

Then he'd stood far too close to her, close enough her voice vibrated inside him, and he could almost taste the subtle scent that clung to her, like sweet, clotted cream sliding down his throat. He'd longed for a hint of that scent since he'd left London, and had recklessly filled his lungs with it this afternoon.

He glanced down at the paper on the table in front of him, at the face his pencil had traced onto the page without his permission. Juliet Templeton gazed back, her lips parted, the corners turned up in that smile he couldn't forget, part wickedness, and part innocence.

What had Juliet seen, when she'd gazed so intently at *his* face?

He'd never laid eyes on the eldest Templeton sister—Euphemia, Juliet had called her—but perhaps Euphemia had always insisted on being the time-keeper because she hadn't wanted to know how others saw her. Perhaps she hadn't dared to be *seen*, any more than he did.

But there was no unseeing Juliet, the arch of her cheekbones, the curve of her chin, the long, graceful neck—there was sensuality in every line of her face, every angle, every bit of shading, his fascination with her as obvious as if he'd written verses to her instead of merely drawing her.

And her eyes... her *eyes*.

He traced his fingertip around one, the lid and the fringe of dark lashes, the slight upturn at the top corners, and the color, that deep, pure blue, oceans and skies... he covered the face on the page with his hand, but there was no escaping that face in his mind's eye.

There hadn't been, from the start.

"Let's see your sketch, Cross."

He jerked his head up to find Barnaby standing over him, his own drawing clutched in one hand and the other held out for Miles's page. "No, it's, ah... it's not very good. How did you do, cousin?"

Barnaby hesitated, then shot a glance across the room at Lady Cora, his cheeks coloring when he found her gaze on him. "Oh, well enough, I suppose."

Ah. That shy little exchange of glances looked so promising, some of Miles's dark, brooding mood lifted. "Let's see it, then."

"I think it looks rather like her." Barnaby handed over his sketch. "Her eyes and chin, and her... er, her lips."

Miles folded his own sketch and slipped it into his

pocket, then took Barnaby's and smoothed it out on the table in front of him. His cousin was no artist, any more than he was himself, but anyone could see from his drawing that he'd spent time studying Lady Cora's face, and more time still trying to capture it.

"It does look like her, very much." He handed the paper back to Barnaby. "She was a pretty little girl, and she's grown into a lovely young lady."

"She's a perfect angel." Barnaby cast a yearning glance across the room, where Lady Cora sat with her mother, Lady Fosberry, and Juliet, all four of them admiring each other's drawings. "Rather a pleasant way to pass an afternoon, eh, Cross? I don't say it compares to grouse hunting, but it was diverting, for all that. It was clever of Miss Templeton to think of it."

Juliet *was* clever. Too clever, and too... *everything*. Too distracting, too provoking, and too beautiful. Every instinct of self-preservation screamed at him to toss her out his front door and let the wind and rain blow her back to London, before it was too late for him.

But it was already too late, wasn't it?

Six days. Six short days, and he was already thinking of her as Juliet again, despite his every effort not to think of her at all. Somehow, without his permission she'd become Juliet in his mind, if not on his lips—

"Stop that incessant glowering, Cross." Barnaby frowned at him. "Do you suppose Miss Templeton doesn't notice that every time you look at her, you're glaring?"

"Don't be absurd. I'm not glaring at Miss Templeton."

Miles tore his gaze away from her, but a moment

later it was already wandering back to her again. He was helpless to resist the temptation of that face.

She was studying the sketch she'd done of *him*— he knew it, somehow, though he didn't know how he could, since he couldn't see her paper. Perhaps it was the puzzled expression on her face, as if she couldn't quite make sense of what she was seeing.

Miles forced his attention back to Barnaby. "How is Lady Cora's sketch of you? Did she do you justice?"

Barnaby grinned. "More than justice. I never realized I was such a handsome devil."

Miles snorted. "All the Cross men are uncommonly handsome, Barnaby."

"Miss Templeton seems to think *you* are." Barnaby gave him a sly nudge.

"Does she?" Miles followed his cousin's glance, his own catching and holding on Juliet's face, as it always did whenever he risked a look at her.

"Yes. I can't think what she sees in an unpleasant fellow like you, Cross, but there's no denying there's a certain... affection in her portrayal of you. Warmth, even."

Warmth? No, surely not. "You're mistaken, cousin."

"Not a bit of it, Cross. Have a look at her sketch yourself, if you don't believe me." Barnaby took up his drawing of Lady Cora, slid it into his coat pocket, then gave Miles a friendly slap on the back. "I'm off to escort Lady Cora and her mother through the portrait gallery. They expressed a desire to see it, though I can't think why. There's nothing to see but a bunch of dull portraits of fusty old Cross earls and countesses."

Miles nodded, but Barnaby's ramblings slipped meaninglessly through his ears.

All of his attention was once again absorbed by Juliet Templeton.

Her sketch of him... he wanted to see it.

No. It was more than that, worse than that.

He *needed* to see it.

Burned to see it.

Yet what good would come of it? He'd see her sketch, and then what? She'd demand to see his sketch of her, and it would only delay the inevitable end of this strange attraction between them. With every word they exchanged, every furtive glance between them, he slipped a little further under the surface.

Soon enough, he'd be drowning in her again.

But even as these dark thoughts wound through his head, he was winding his way across the room, bypassing his other guests with hardly a glance, his gaze full of *her*.

Always her.

"Miss Templeton. May I have a word?"

She gave him such a wary look he caught her wrist—*again*, because he couldn't seem to stop touching her—to forestall a refusal, but before she could say a word, Lady Fosberry gave Juliet a tranquil smile and a little pat on the shoulder. "Go on, dearest. I fancy a rest before it's time to dress for supper."

Juliet shook her head, her blue eyes wide. "Oh, but I don't think—"

"Nonsense, child. Lord Cross *is* our host, you know, and in any case, I'm certain he only wishes to thank you for suggesting such a clever game to entertain his guests this afternoon. Isn't that right, Lord Cross?" Lady Fosberry raised an eyebrow at him.

"Yes, of course, my lady."

"He can thank me right—"

He whisked her away before she could protest further, hurrying her from the drawing room, through the entryway and down the adjacent hallway toward his study.

"For pity's sake, Lord Cross, there's no need to drag me!"

She snatched at her hand, and he released her, but he closed the study door behind them, and leaned his back against it.

"If you've quite finished manhandling me, Lord Cross, then—"

"Show me your sketch."

"What? I certainly will not!"

"Oh, but you will, Juliet." He gathered a lock of her hair in his hand, stifling a groan at the dark, silky drag of it, as if he'd caught a ribbon of midnight on his fingertips. "I'm afraid I must insist."

"You're mad." Her eyes widened as he wrapped the lock of her hair around his fingers and gently drew her closer, then closer still. Her gaze darted toward the door behind him, but unless she wanted to climb him like a tree, there was no escape that way.

He released his hold on her hair when she began to back away, but he followed her, and soon enough she came up against the long length of his desk behind her. "Lord Cross—"

"Show me your sketch." He advanced on her slowly, his footsteps thudding in time with his thundering heartbeat. God, he'd gone mad, prowling after her like this. But he kept going, his gaze trapped by the frantic fluttering of her pulse in the pale hollow of her throat. "Show me your sketch, Juliet."

"No! How dare you? I don't have to show you anything."

He was upon her now, close enough he drew her scent inside himself with every breath, vanilla warmed by her skin, a delicate flush of color across her cheeks, and that pulse point at her neck fluttering wildly...

"Shall I show you mine, then?" He reached into the pocket of his coat and pulled the folded paper out. "Do you want to know what I see when I look at you, Juliet?"

"No, I..." She pressed her hand over her throat. "No."

"Liar." She did want to see it, was leaning closer to him even now, perhaps without realizing it, her throat working, her eyes as blue as the last moments of twilight, just before the sun sinks below the horizon, and the sky turns its darkest, deepest shade before it fades to black.

Except they weren't just blue, were they? They were flecked with gold, like tiny stars scattered in a midnight sky, so tiny one wouldn't notice them unless they were as close to her as he was now.

Had he ever been this close to her? So unbearably, intoxicatingly close...

"Such blue, blue eyes." He touched her chin, raising her face to his. "I've never seen eyes as blue as yours."

A furrow appeared on that smooth, white brow. "Well, you needn't sound so put out about it."

"But I *am* put out, Juliet." He couldn't stop staring at her mouth. He reached out to trace his thumb over her pouting lower lip, and every part of his body went tight, every inch of him clenched and aching from the glide of the red, petal-soft flesh under his fingertip.

"Are you... going to k-kiss me, Lord Cross?"

Was he? It was madness for him to kiss a lady who addressed him so formally, as if they'd never sat beside each other in a carriage, their thighs pressed together, or walked down a narrow pathway in a lush rose garden, side by side, the backs of her gloved fingers brushing his.

Had he really believed he could forget her? Every touch, every word, every smile they'd shared, he remembered it all, and he was selfish—so selfish, because he *wanted* her, even knowing he didn't deserve her.

But he no longer cared, because she was gazing up at him with those sleepy, dark blue eyes, and he was sliding his fingers under her chin, her skin softer than a whisper, and raising her face to his so he could take her mouth.

Deeply. Wet. The way he'd wanted to since he'd first heard that sultry voice, the edge of impudence that made him want to nip at her, taste the pertness of her tongue.

She didn't pull away, but urged him closer, the soft curves of her breasts pressing against his chest. "If you do intend to kiss me, Lord Cross, then I suggest you get on with it."

It was a tease, yes—she was the only woman who'd ever dared tease him—but it was an invitation, too, and he could refuse her nothing.

The second his lips met hers, every inch of his skin and the hair on the back of his neck leapt to life, though the kiss was gentle, restrained.

At first.

But it wasn't long before he was sliding his tongue against the seam of her lips, tormented by that hint of damp heat.

Not enough...

Her chest moved against his in a long, slow, warm drift of her breath against his lips, and then she parted for him.

Once he was inside, every thought fled, except one.

More.

"Yes." She toyed with the hair at the back of his neck, sifting it through her fingers. "Please, more."

Had he said it aloud? There was no time to answer that question—hardly time to ask it—before he was drowning in her. He eased her backward, so she was pressed against his desk, then closed his hands around her waist and lifted her onto the wide, smooth surface. A few letters drifted to the floor, but he didn't care.

He didn't *care.*

She let out a soft gasp, as if surprised, but she remained where she was, her face tipped up to his. Her lips were redder than usual, a trifle swollen from his kiss, and he let out a pained groan as his cock jerked against his falls.

A shiver went through her when he took her mouth again, his tongue stroking hers with gentle insistence, then harder, demanding a response, his restraint crumbling with every heated drift of her breath.

"Closer," he growled against her lips.

She rested a hand on his chest. "Any closer, my lord, and you'll be on my lap."

He choked out a laugh, and paused to run his

tongue up the silky skin of her neck and behind her ear, soft vanilla invading his senses, and making him dizzy with desire. "You smell so good," he murmured, low in her ear, then closed his teeth around her earlobe.

She gasped, her other hand flying to his chest. "Did you just... bite me?"

"It was more of a nibble, really." He did it again, taking her soft, plump lobe between his lips, teasing her until she was sighing in his arms, then he slid his hands down to her curved hips, holding her still as he scraped his teeth gently down her throat.

She sucked in another breath at the caress. "Oh, that... it feels so strange."

He touched his fingertip to the shallow indentation in the center of her chin, the dimple so tiny it would be imperceptible to anyone whose whole attention wasn't fixed on her face.

But his was. He'd noticed that dimple the first time he'd seen her. After that, nothing about the lines of her face had gone unnoticed by him. He'd studied every arch, every curve, and learned every subtlety of the geometry of her face.

"Tell me to stop, Juliet." If she didn't push him away, he'd be mad enough to keep kissing her...

"What if I don't want you to stop?"

"You should want it." Already he was hard and aching for her, every instinct screaming at him to push her knees apart and make a home for himself between her thighs. He traced his finger over her lush lower lip, then let it trail down her long, slender neck until it came to a stop between her breasts.

She made a sound then, a hushed breath, or a throaty sigh, perhaps, but she didn't push him away

—just gazed up at him with those blue eyes that haunted him, not a single thing about her expression warning him there was a line beyond which she would not permit him to cross.

Good Lord, but she was dangerous, to his body, and to his heart.

Without warning, his fingers tightened around her hips and he jerked her closer to the edge of the desk, only his thighs and the bulk of his body keeping her from toppling forward onto the floor. He caught her wrists and raised them to his shoulders. "Put your arms around my neck."

She did as he bid her, but hid her eyes behind her long, thick eyelashes.

"No, Juliet." He raised her chin. "Look at me."

"I see you, my lord. I have from the start." She peeked up at him from under her lashes, a glitter of blue fire behind that lush, dark fringe, a tease and a temptation, yes, but she'd never been the seductress he'd once told himself she was.

She'd never been anyone other than herself.

She let out a soft moan when he kissed her again, his lips insistent against hers, his tongue seeking entry, a swell of triumph rising in his chest when she opened for him at once, welcoming him into that dark pink heat.

This time, he left no corner of her mouth untouched, but drifted into every secret hollow, tasted every curve, his senses swimming with the scent of her, his tongue alive with the flavor of sweet cream.

CHAPTER
ELEVEN

Juliet had been kissed once before, when she was eight years old.

One of her father's friends had brought his son on a visit to Hambleden Manor, and the boy had kissed her on the cheek. It had been quick and sweet, and they'd both blushed furiously afterwards.

Miles's kiss wasn't sweet. It wasn't even a kiss so much as a claiming—a pulse-leaping, heart-fluttering, dizzying *taking* that blazed through her like a conflagration, sending a shower of sparks through every nerve ending, seizing her breath from her lungs, and stealing her reason.

His mouth was dark heat, the wild, rich taste of him melting on her tongue.

"Open for me, Juliet."

A delicious little thrill tripped down her spine at the rough demand, and she obeyed him instinctively, gasping when he surged into her mouth and slid the slick tip of his tongue across the inside of her bottom lip.

He knew, somehow, just how to kiss her, how to use his lips, his tongue and his teeth... God in heaven, the gentle rasp of his *teeth*... to stoke the smoldering heat in her lower belly until she was straining against him, her knees pressed against his hips and her fingers in his hair, tugging, pulling him closer. "Miles..."

"Shh. I've got you." His wide palms slid down the outside of her thighs to her knees, easing them up so he could press closer between her legs... yes, please, *yes*, her bottom sliding over the slippery surface of his desk until her hips collided with his, his possessive hands holding her tightly against him, and...

Dear God, she could *feel* him, hot and hard, even with the layers of clothing between them, and his *voice*, low and dark and filthy in her ear, urging her on, his teeth worrying her earlobe, a tiny sharp bite that made her shudder against him, dragging a groan from his throat.

He cupped her breast in his palm and stroked her nipple with his thumb, slow, sinuous circles, his mouth so hot on her throat, her neck arching, her head falling back in invitation.

"*Juliet.*" It was a growl, a command and a plea at once, the cool air on the heated skin of her back as her buttons gave way to the frantic tug of his fingers, his other hand fisting her skirts, dragging them up past her knees, her thighs. "Want you."

And she... oh, she wanted so many things, dreamt so many dreams still, just as she'd done when she was a girl, but she didn't want anything as badly as she wanted him. "Then take me, my lord."

Because it should be that simple, shouldn't it? As simple as wanting him, and lying back for him, her spine against the polished wood of his desk, her hand on his neck, his pulse beating against her fingertips as he wrestled with the buttons of his falls—

Until suddenly he froze, listening, his fingers pressed to her lips. "Someone's coming."

A moment later, she heard it, too, voices in the entryway, mere steps from the study, and then, growing louder with each of her panting breaths, footsteps echoing down the corridor.

"Quickly." Miles grasped her upper arms and lifted her upright, wrestling with the back of her gown until he'd closed every button that he'd opened with such desperation only moments before. Then with one quick tug he slid her off the desk and into a chair, buttoned his falls, and strode over to the window behind his desk, his back to her.

That's where they were when Lord Barnaby strode into the study a moment later. "Ah, Cross. I've been looking for you. I wanted to ask if you..." he trailed off, glancing between the two of them. "What's happened *now*?"

"I don't know what you mean." Miles didn't turn from the window. "Nothing's happened. What do you *want*, Barnaby?"

Barnaby cleared his throat. "I came to enquire, cousin, whether or not you expected Lord Boggs to appear at Steeple Cross."

"Boggs?" Miles did turn then, his eyebrows raised. "God, no. Don't tell me he's—"

"Here? I'm afraid so, cousin, and regrettably, Mrs. Poole's already shown him into the drawing room."

"How unfortunate." Miles gave his coat a sharp tug. "Very well. I'll see to him."

"Wait, Cross. He didn't ask for you. He, ah..." Barnaby cast her an uneasy glance. "That's the strange thing. He's asking to see Miss Templeton."

"*Me*?" What in the world did Lord Boggs want

with *her*? "I don't understand. Are you quite certain he asked for me, Lord Barnaby?"

"I am, indeed. He claims you told him you'd be at Steeple Cross when he came to call on you at Lady Fosberry's the day before you left London for Oxfordshire, and... well, he seems to be under the impression you, ah... invited him to join you here."

"*I* invited him?" Why, what did the man *mean*, telling Lord Barnaby she'd invited him to Steeple Cross? All of London might think her a shameless adventuress, but she wasn't so lost to propriety she'd make an assignation with one gentleman at another gentleman's house!

"You *are* acquainted with Lord Boggs, I believe, Miss Templeton?" There was nothing accusatory in Miles's voice, but the look he gave her was decidedly cool.

"Well, yes. Everyone in London is acquainted with Lord Boggs." It was true enough, but a guilty heat was creeping into her cheeks, nonetheless.

The trouble was, she *had* encouraged Lord Boggs's attentions to her when she'd first arrived in London, foolishly thinking his hunt for a bride might coincide with her wish to save her family from penury with an advantageous marriage.

But that had been weeks ago, and it wasn't as if anything inappropriate had happened between them. Surely, the man couldn't have mistaken a few smiles and a dance or two for an invitation to chase her to Steeple Cross?

"Did you see him the day before you left London?"

Another lady might have believed Miles spoke with perfect courtesy, but she'd heard that tone before, and knew it for the thin veneer of courtesy it was.

She raised her chin, and met his eyes. "I did see him, yes. He called on Lady Fosberry, but I never—"

"I see." Miles turned away from her. "Would you be so good as to take Miss Templeton to the drawing room, Barnaby?"

Barnaby glanced between them again, his expression troubled. "Cross—"

"It's quite all right, cousin. Miss Templeton and I have concluded our business." Miles waved his hand toward the door in a clear dismissal, as if she were one of his servants.

She remained frozen in place, her skin still tingling from his touch, unable to squeak out another word.

To see him now, she could almost believe she'd imagined his heated kisses, his touch, his whispers in her ear. The passionate man of only moments before was gone, and in his place was the cool, dignified Earl of Cross, with his perfectly tied cravat, his every button fastened, and every lock of his dark hair smoothed into its proper place.

What had just happened?

"Go on, Miss Templeton." The cool, dark eyes met hers. "You don't want to keep Lord Boggs waiting."

"Very well, my lord." She rose from her chair with icy dignity—at least, she hoped it was dignified, and icy enough to give him frostbite—because she hadn't done anything wrong, and she wouldn't sneak away in shame as if she had.

But her performance was wasted on Miles. He'd turned back to the window, and wasn't even looking at her anymore.

Well then, there was no reason for her to remain here a moment longer, was there? Without another word, she swept out the door, Lord Barnaby on her heels, without sparing the infuriating Earl of Cross another glance.

~

"Miss Templeton, my dear girl, here you are at last, and as lovely as ever!" Lord Boggs offered her an ingratiating bow, then caught her hand and pressed an oily kiss to her knuckles.

"Er, thank you, my lord." It took every bit of restraint she possessed, but somehow Juliet was able to wait until he released her instead of snatching it away from him. "What a surprise to see you here, my lord. How did you manage the journey in such dreadful weather?"

For pity's sake, what use was a tempest if it couldn't keep Lord Boggs from descending on Oxfordshire?

He peered down his bulbous nose at her, a smug smile on his lips. "A superior equipage and driver, and the best horses England has to offer, Miss Templeton."

"Of course." She stretched a smile over her clenched teeth. "Have you just come from London, then?"

"Yes. I intended to be here sooner, but some rather, er... pressing business kept me in town longer than I wished. It's dreadfully dull there, now all the *ton* has left the city. Indeed, I believe all the fashionable people are *here*." He glanced around him with a haughty sniff. "Quite a distance to come for a bit of hunting, really. I confess I don't see the appeal."

That hadn't stopped *him* from coming here though, had it?

There was no reason his condescension should offend her—this wasn't *her* house, after all, and it wasn't as if she admired Steeple Cross—but before she could think better of it, she'd opened her mouth to defend it. "It's a handsome house, and the surrounding park is quite—"

"Shall we take a walk in the conservatory before dinner, Miss Templeton? I hear Cross has a rather nice one, if a trifle small." He offered her his arm without waiting for her reply.

The conservatory was as good—or, rather, as *bad* a place as any other, so she accepted his arm without argument, only pausing to mutter a quick prayer that they wouldn't encounter Lady Cecil or her nieces, or Lord and Lady Kimble and their daughters wandering about in there.

Thankfully, it was empty, but there was precious little else to be thankful for, as the conservatory was an orchestrated nightmare, just like every other place at Steeple Cross.

Every stem was straight, every leaf upright, every flower, shrub and bush trimmed to merciless perfection. It was no less than she'd expected, really, yet somehow the coldness of this place, the ruthless sterility was much more disturbing to her *here* than it ever could be in a breakfast parlor or bedchamber.

Her father had been a botanist, his knowledge so comprehensive he could identify thousands of plants by species, genus, family, and order, and even *his* gardens hadn't been as perfectly ordered as these were.

Plants, flowers, growing things... they were meant to live in wild profusion, in a riot of tender greens and bright pinks and deep, ruby reds. There should be loose dirt overflowing onto the pathways, fallen petals gathering on the ground, and dried leaves that caught in one's skirt as they passed by, just like at her family's small gardens at Hambleden Manor.

She paused to run her fingertips over a lovely, royal purple dahlia, its ruffled petals tipped in pure white, spiraling from a yellow center like a starburst, and all at once a crushing sadness rolled over her, like a grim, dark cloud shutting out the sunlight and stealing every lingering bit of warmth, and... oh, it was unbearable, this wretched place, and dear God, were those *tears* stinging her eyes?

"Are you aware Lord Melrose is in London, Miss Templeton?"

Lord Melrose, in *London*? She halted in the middle of the pathway, alarm fluttering in her chest. What in the world was Lord Melrose doing in London? He was meant to be in Buckinghamshire, wooing Emmeline! "Is he, indeed? How does Lord Melrose do?"

A tiny, inexplicable smirk curled the corners of Lord Boggs's lips. "Not well at all, I'm afraid. Indeed, he appeared to me to be a trifle despondent."

"That's a pity, my lord. I'm sorry for him." *Oh, no.* What had happened? Had Emmeline refused poor Lord Melrose once and for all, and sent him back to London with a broken heart?

"Yes, it's all quite terrible. I can't say for certain, of course, as I am not in Lord Melrose's confidence, but I believe I heard something about his being disappointed in love."

"Disappointed?" Was it finished between him and

Emmeline, then? Had she put an end to his courtship, and her sisters were afraid to tell her? Was that why Euphemia hadn't written?

"Oh, dear. I see I've upset you, Miss Templeton. I'm desolated to give you even a moment's concern, but it's likely all gossip, without a shred of truth to it. I daresay you'd know better than I possibly could how things go between your sister and Lord Melrose."

But she *didn't* know. She didn't know a blessed thing, and what other explanation could there be for the resounding silence from her sisters, if the worst hadn't happened? What would become of Emmeline *now*, and poor Lord Melrose, who'd offered himself to her so earnestly, and been so hopeful all would come right in the end?

"My dear Miss Templeton, I see you are greatly distressed, and I most humbly beg your pardon for my carelessness, but surely you know all hope is not lost?" He took her hand, and pressed his thumb into the center of her palm. "I promise you all will work out as it's meant to in the end."

This time, she did wrench her hand from his, her stomach roiling at the familiarity of his touch, the suggestiveness of it. "Forgive me, Lord Boggs, but I find myself rather fatigued, and must return to my bedchamber."

She had to find Lady Fosberry at once. Her ladyship would know what to do.

"But of course, Miss Templeton. A rest will do you wonders, I'm certain." He offered her another preening bow, a gleam in his watery blue eyes. "Until dinner, then, my dear."

CHAPTER
TWELVE

"What delightful giblet soup this is, Lord Cross! Really, my lord, can you think of a single thing in the world more pleasing than a tender giblet?"

Hundreds of things, chief among them, *silence*.

"And such delicious vegetables! I'm certain I've never tasted more flavorful stewed peas than these, my lord, and these partridges are perfectly divine!"

Lady Cecil's eldest niece was flirting with him. Either that, or she was having some sort of fit. It was difficult to tell which.

How the girl—a chit whose name he couldn't have remembered if he'd had a pistol pointed at his temple—had ended up seated to his right at the table was a puzzle, likely orchestrated by the same dark forces who'd seen to it Juliet was seated as far away from him as physically possible, while they yet remained in the same room.

She was tucked so thoroughly away at the other end of the table he'd have to stand atop his chair to see her. Perhaps he would have, manners be damned if she'd looked in his direction even once throughout the entire meal, but she hadn't.

Nor did she look at anyone else.

She sat quietly, her face pale, and her gaze fixed on her plate. She hardly ate a thing, despite the efforts of Lord Boggs, who was seated beside her, and paying her such marked attention Miles nearly overturned the dining table just to make it *stop*.

"Why, I'm perfectly *mad* for boiled mushrooms! Aren't you, Lord Cross?"

"Not in the least." No one was mad for boiled mushrooms, for God's sake.

But the more liberally his dinner partner partook of the wine served with each course, the more enthusiastic she became, and the more determined to engage his attention. His head was pounding by the time the second courses were brought in, and she... what the *devil* was her name? was shrieking about—

"Eels! Why, I've never tasted such mouthwatering eels, and these artichoke bottoms! Have you ever had nicer artichoke bottoms in your life, Aunt?"

"No, indeed!" Lady Cecil was more shrill than usual, her voice echoing in every corner of the dining room. "Do you keep a French chef, Lord Cross? I daresay you must, for no English cook could have produced plumper artichoke bottoms than *yours*, my lord!"

He didn't have a word to say on the subject of artichoke bottoms, so he said nothing, but his silence didn't discourage Lady Cecil and her niece, who regaled him with eager compliments from one arduous hour to the next, while his footmen carried in dish after cursed dish, until dinner had dragged on into an eternity.

He'd never spent a more miserable evening in his life.

By the time the final course had been cleared and the ladies had retired to the drawing room, he seized his chance, and rose to his feet. "You'll see to the gentlemen for a while, won't you, Barnaby?"

Barnaby turned to him, startled. "What, you're leaving the table? You're the host, Cross! You can't simply wander away when you grow bored."

"If I'd left when I grew bored, cousin, I'd have gone before the soup was cleared. I've a matter of some importance to attend to, but I'll return soon enough. In the meantime, you may as well become accustomed to acting as host."

"What the *devil* are you on about? You can't truly mean to—"

But he *did* mean to. He turned on his heel before Barnaby could object further, strode from the room without another word and made his way toward the drawing room, leaving his poor cousin with his mouth hanging open.

Alas, it was a wasted effort. Juliet was trapped on a settee near the front of the room, firmly wedged between Lady Fosberry and Lady Drummond. He'd have an easier time liberating a murderer from Newgate than he would discreetly stealing her away.

If he were as devoted a cousin as he should be, he'd return to the dining room at once to relieve Barnaby of the task he'd given him, but for now, perhaps the wider a berth he kept between himself and Boggs, the better. Otherwise the man could well find himself on his way back to London tonight, the abominable weather be damned.

So, he retreated to the blessed quiet of his study,

instead. Once he was there, he poured himself a glass of port, then dropped down into a chair before the fire with a sigh too deep to have been torn from anywhere other than the murkiest depths of his chest.

He'd made a mess of things with Juliet, in every way in which a gentleman could make a mess of things with a lady. For instance, a proper gentleman did not *devour* a lady's lips as he'd done to Juliet's lips this afternoon, and he certainly didn't plunk her down on top of his desk, hike up her skirts, and insinuate himself between her thighs.

Good Lord, what had he been thinking? For all her natural sensuality, Juliet was an *innocent*, for God's sake. He should have considered that before he kissed her, urged her lips to part under his, felt the softness of them, the warmth inside, the taste of her...

But his appalling lack of control wasn't even the worst of his sins.

She hadn't invited Lord Boggs to attend her here at Steeple Cross. No one who'd seen her at dinner tonight could possibly imagine she longed for Boggs's company. Unfortunately, he hadn't reached this conclusion until the hot streak of jealousy in his chest had cooled, and he'd been able to consider the matter rationally.

Jealous and irrational, over a lady he didn't deserve, and could never have.

She'd felt his coldness this afternoon, and had understood every one of the veiled accusations he'd flung at her. He owed her an apology, but tomorrow would have to be soon enough to beg her pardon. Until then, he'd make do with another glass of port. Perhaps it would help soothe his guilt.

Or perhaps two glasses would.

Just as he'd raised the glass to his lips, however, the door to his study burst open, and Barnaby appeared in front of him, looking like a thundercloud. "What did you mean, I may as well get accustomed to acting as host? I demand to know at once, Cross."

Miles took a sip of his port before he glanced up at his cousin. "What's become of my guests? You agreed to look after them, Barnaby."

"Bollocks. I never agreed to a thing, as you're well aware. They're content enough, as long as the port and cigars hold out. It smells like a bloody gaming hell in there already." Barnaby helped himself to a glass of port, then plopped down into a chair across from Miles.

"I don't recall inviting you to join me, cousin."

"That's too bloody bad, Cross. I'm here now, and I've no intention of leaving until I've had my say."

God in heaven, was he to have no peace? "Be quick about it, then."

"Very well. How long do you intend to keep up the charade that you're not madly in love with Juliet Templeton?"

In love with Juliet Templeton, indeed! The very idea is preposterous! You only imagine so because you're in love with Lady Cora, and think every other gentleman must feel as you do—

The denials all rushed to his lips at once, but the healthy draught of port he'd just swallowed rushed into his lungs, leading to a coughing fit that prevented him from uttering a single word of it. Then, somewhere between his denials and a near-fatal gagging, the strangest thing happened.

He no longer *wanted* to deny it. He had to tell someone, as he was making a bloody mess of it on his own, and if he couldn't tell the truth to Barnaby, who could he tell? He swirled the remainder of the port in his glass, tossed it back in one swallow, and met his cousin's eyes. "It doesn't matter if I'm in love with Juliet or not, Barnaby. She isn't for me."

"Bollocks, Cross. Why shouldn't she be for you?"

"I don't intend to marry, ever. I'm... not suited for it."

He'd always thought this perfectly obvious, but Barnaby's eyebrows shot into his hairline as if he'd never heard anything more ridiculous. "*Now* what are you on about, Cross?"

"Look around you, cousin." Miles waved his glass around. "If you were Miss Templeton—or any young lady, come to that—would you want to live here? Damn it," he muttered, when the port sloshed over the side of his glass and splattered the cuff of his shirt.

"Then bring her to one of your other dozen or so houses."

"Where, Barnaby? My country seat in Kent? Don't you recall how miserable my mother was there?"

"Well, perhaps not *there*, but one of the others—"

"They're all the same, Barnaby, but it isn't even the houses, it's..."

"What?" Carefully, Barnaby set his glass aside. "What is it, Cross?"

Miles stared at the drops of port he'd spilled, the dark red against the spotless white linen. "Don't you recall how miserable he made her?"

Barnaby sighed. "I recall it, yes, but what does your father's heartlessness have to do with *you* being in love with Miss Templeton?"

"When a gentleman is in love with a lady, he marries her, Barnaby." Miles didn't bother with a glass this time, but lifted the bottle directly to his lips.

"Yes, I believe I've heard something to that effect, but you still haven't answered my question, Cross."

"Only the worst sort of scoundrel would take a lady like Juliet Templeton and doom her to a lifetime with a man who doesn't have the first idea how to behave as a husband should. That would be like... like trapping a bright, colorful songbird in a cage until she no longer sings."

Until she became so despondent, she lost her song forever.

"Don't look at me like that, Barnaby." Miles took another gulp from the bottle. "It's nothing more than the truth."

"Bollocks. It's nowhere near the truth. You're *nothing* at all like your father was, Cross. He was bloody terrifying. Do you know I was frightened to death of him as a child?"

"I was, too, and so was she." His mother had been a quiet, tender-hearted lady, and no match for her harsh, exacting husband. He'd lectured and tormented her until he'd whittled her down to a bleak shadow of the happy, pink-cheeked lady she'd once been. She'd shrunk further into herself with every year that passed.

Until finally, she'd disappeared altogether.

"Yes, but I've never been terrified of *you*, Cross. Oh, you're a bit rigid, rather like an over-starched cravat, not to mention moody and occasionally ill-tempered—"

"Is there a point forthcoming, Barnaby?"

"The point, cousin, is despite your flaws, you're a good, decent man. You've always been patient with me, and you're an excellent friend to Melrose. Why would you think you wouldn't be a fine husband, as well?"

Because people didn't change. Not really. Especially when they hadn't the first idea what to change into. "It's too late for that, Barnaby."

"Bollocks. You're only forty years old, Cross—"

"Twenty-nine." He raised the bottle to his lips again. "And stop saying bollocks. It's vulgar."

"Then stop forcing me to say it with this nonsense. Instead of engaging in these Byronic histrionics, you'd do well to send up a prayer of thanks to the heavens for sending you a lady as ideally suited to you as Juliet Templeton."

"You're mad, cousin. We don't suit at all." Juliet was playing-at-bowls-in-a-ballroom, rearranging-all-the-books-in-the-library chaotic. "She's... chaotic."

Delightfully, unpredictably, joyously chaotic, and he was stiff, starched, pressed, and perfectly creased. How could he ever do justice to such a magnificent tumult of a wife? He couldn't even bring himself to wear a scarlet waistcoat embroidered with golden suns, for God's sake.

"You could do with more chaos in your life, Cross. Think about it. I'm back off to the dining room, before those villains you left in there empty every bottle of port in the cellars."

"As long as they leave me this one." Miles curled a protective arm around his own bottle.

Barnaby rose to his feet, but he paused at the door. "What did you mean earlier, when you said I'd better grow accustomed to acting as host?"

"That? Only that you'll take on more of the duties

of the earldom once you and Lady Cora marry. I despise company, as you know, Barnaby, and I don't mean to entertain, or spend much time in town in the future."

"What, you mean to hole up here at Steeple Cross, like a lonely hermit?"

"Not a hermit, cousin, an *eccentric*. That's what they call it when you're an earl."

Barnaby snorted. "If you say so, cousin. But before you decide against doing Juliet Templeton the grievous insult of asking her to be your countess, and thus ruining all her happiness, do one thing for me, will you?"

"Anything, cousin."

"Ask yourself this. Do you believe Juliet will be happier with Lord Boggs than she would be with you? Because that's Boggs is headed, and she isn't in any position to refuse him."

Barnaby didn't wait for an answer, but slipped out the door, leaving Miles alone.

He slunk lower in his chair, clasping his half-empty bottle of port to his chest, but somehow it slipped through the crook of his elbow and dropped onto the floor.

He peered over the arm of his chair, and watched the ruby red river streaming across the pale cream and blue Aubusson under his feet, then slumped back with a sigh. "Bollocks."

CHAPTER
THIRTEEN

"Juliet, dearest, come and sit here next to me, won't you?" Lady Fosberry patted the empty place beside her on the narrow settee she'd commandeered, a claw-footed monstrosity done in a rather sickly canary-colored satin stripe.

Canary satin stripe, of all things, and a pure punishment to sit upon, rather like one of the dreaded pews at St. Peter's Church in Hambleden. But Juliet did as Lady Fosberry bid her, hiding a wince as the hard wood commenced with torturing her backside.

"Now, Lady Drummond, if you'd be so good as to take the seat beside Miss Templeton, with Lady Cora in the chair just there, I'll have nothing more to wish for."

A distressed little grunt escaped poor Lady Drummond as she squeezed onto the settee, and was rewarded for her trouble with an accidental jab in the ribs from Juliet's elbow.

"There!" Lady Fosberry beamed at them. "Isn't this cozy?"

Juliet offered Lady Drummond an apologetic grimace. "I daresay you'd be more comfortable sitting on my lap, my lady."

"Now, you mustn't think of it, Miss Templeton." Lady Drummond patted her hand. "We can't leave you at Lord Boggs's mercy all evening, worrying you with his pointed attentions."

"No, indeed. We saw quite enough of *that* at dinner. I don't know what he's doing here, but I don't like it. I must impress upon you how very much I disapprove of him, Juliet, and I've no doubt your sisters will, as well."

"Yes, my lady." If Juliet hadn't drawn that conclusion the first time Lady Fosberry felt the need to impress it upon her, she certainly had the second, third, and fourth times.

"That dreadful smirk of his!" Lady Drummond shuddered. "Why, who does the man think he is?"

"Very high in the instep, that one. I can't countenance him." Lady Fosberry shot a dark look at the drawing room door, so Lord Boggs might not sneak up on her unawares. "Why, he put me right off my raspberry puffs, and you know how I adore raspberry puffs, Juliet."

"Well, you'll be safe enough there, Miss Templeton." Lady Cora gave Juliet a sympathetic smile before stealing a furtive peek at the door. "How long do you suppose the gentlemen will be at their port this evening?"

"I've a notion they'll be quicker than usual." Juliet raised a knowing eyebrow at Lady Cora. "For a moment when we left the table, it looked as if Lord Barnaby was going to come with us, didn't it, Lady Drummond?"

Lady Drummond laughed, and Lady Cora flushed

up to the roots of her hair. "You're a dreadful tease, Miss Templeton." But her gaze remained pinned on the door, and she wore a dreamy smile on her lips that left little doubt as to the state of her heart.

I did that.

She hadn't, of course, not really. Lady Cora and Lord Barnaby had done it, but she'd helped them along, and as was always the case when one exerted oneself on behalf of a friend, she'd helped herself at the same time, too. It did wonders for her own wavering faith in love to see such a besotted smile on Lady Cora's face.

Still, as the evening stretched on, her optimism began to fade. Neither Lord Barnaby nor Lord Cross appeared in the drawing room with the rest of the gentlemen, and Lady Cora, who'd been so filled with anticipation only moments before deflated like a punctured hot air balloon.

As for Lord Boggs, he was visibly annoyed to find two glowering ladyships flanking her on either side, and took no pains to hide it. He huffed and muttered and glared, Lady Cecil and her nieces whispered and glared, Lady Fosberry and Lady Drummond sniffed and glared—all this while Lord and Lady Kimble's daughters displayed their musical skills by nearly pounding the pianoforte into dust.

At last, she managed to escape by pleading a headache, and was dragging herself up to her bedchamber when Lord Barnaby appeared at the bottom of the stairs and called up to her. "I beg your pardon, Miss Templeton, but there's something I'd like to show you, if you're not too fatigued."

She *was* fatigued, her exhaustion a gnawing ache that had sunk into the very depths of her bones, but she was fond of Lord Barnaby, and he was so very earnest in his appeal, she couldn't refuse him. "Yes, of course, my lord, if you wish."

He bounded up the stairs and led her to the long, wide corridor on the second floor that served as Steeple Cross's portrait gallery. There weren't many paintings here, as most of the family portraits were hung in the grand gallery at the country seat in Kent, but even from such a small sampling of faces, one couldn't help but notice the Cross ancestors were a trifle... glum?

By glum, she meant *grim*, each frozen countenance more disapproving than the last, and the countesses weren't much better than the earls. Goodness, was it necessary for aristocrats to be so joyless? Two dozen faces, and not a single smile amongst them.

"The Winthrop family are a somber lot, aren't they?"

"Would you call them *somber*, Miss Templeton?" Lord Barnaby paused beside a portrait of a pinched-looking gentleman in a coat stiff with heavy gold braiding, who was glaring down upon them from a heavy, dark frame. "I'd call them terrifying, but I imagine you're too polite to use such a word."

"Perhaps, but I wouldn't call them welcoming, either." She strolled down the long, wood-paneled corridor, eying the former Earls of Cross as she passed, but so many pairs of dull, dark eyes following her soon became unnerving, so she turned her attention to the intricately-carved gilt frames instead, uncertain whether to admire them, or pity the poor housemaids doomed to eliminate every speck of dust from the tiny curls and spirals.

They were all spotless, of course. Dust wasn't permitted at Steeple Cross.

It was a gloomy place at night, with shadows lingering in every corner. The only source of natural light was a large, triple-paned window tucked between two thick columns at the far end of the room, but it was swallowed by the dark paneling that surrounded it, as well as an enormous stained-glass crest that dominated the entire length of the middle panel.

Even with the sun shining, that window wouldn't do much to eliminate the gloom surrounding them. Dark. Everything here was so utterly, unrelentingly *dark*.

"There aren't many portraits of children." She returned the glacial stare of some dour countess or other in a tight lace cap, who was scowling down at her with a pair of cold, dark eyes.

They were Miles's eyes, except his weren't anywhere near so cold and unfriendly, for all that he occasionally tried to make them so.

"No, the Winthrops haven't proved particularly fruitful. Pity, isn't it? I daresay a passel of frolicsome children might have livened them up a bit, but the Countesses of Cross have been rather frail creatures, on the whole. A great many of them died young, you see. Here's Cross's father." Lord Barnaby nodded at a portrait at the end of the corridor, nearest the window.

"Does Lord Cross favor his father?" Juliet made her way past the row of expressionless faces to join Lord Barnaby, but when she reached his side and glanced up at the portrait, a shudder tripped down her spine. "Oh. Oh, dear."

The previous Earl of Cross had tight lips, a rigid

posture, and a frigid, uncompromising stare so arctic even the painted version chilled one to the soul.

"Frightening, isn't he? His behavior was much like you'd expect from a man of his appearance. My own father was much like him—at least, what I remember of him. He died when I was three. I was raised by an exceedingly tender-hearted mother who spoiled me shamelessly. I was far more fortunate than my cousin was."

Just looking at the Sixth Earl of Cross was twisting her stomach into knots, yet that frigid face held her captive somehow, a thrall of horror, and she couldn't manage to tear her gaze free of it. "He doesn't look like a doting father."

"Far from it. Cross was left to his sole care from the age of nine, when his mother passed away."

Nine? So young, but then it wasn't difficult to believe such a man as his father could drive a woman into an early grave.

"I used to spend the summer months with them at their estate in Kent, and even at a very young age I realized how utterly grim an existence Cross led with his father. I don't think he spoke to another child from the end of each summer to the start of the next."

She swallowed, but the lump in her throat clung like cockleburs. For a little boy to be trapped at a remote estate in Kent with such a father, without another child within miles, and not a single soul aside from servants to speak to? "But that's... dear God, how dreadful it must have been for him."

"It was, yes. I'm afraid he was terribly lonely."

He must have been, unbearably so, and inconceivably so to her, who'd always been surrounded by her sisters, had always basked in their warmth and love.

Even after her mother fled to the Continent with her lover, Lord Bromley, abandoning them all without a backwards glance—even after her father's death, when things had become so difficult, she'd never been *alone*.

What must it have been like for Miles, to have no one?

And wasn't he still alone, in all the ways that mattered? Shut up here at Steeple Cross, in this flawless house, everything polished to a ruthless shine, and shelves upon shelves of books so orderly one was afraid to touch them?

"His upbringing followed him to school and beyond." Lord Barnaby let out a long sigh. "I'd hoped when he escaped his father's house things would improve for him, but he... well, he didn't make friends easily, either at Eton or Oxford. Even now he doesn't have many truly close friends, aside from Melrose. I think he just... well, he doesn't know how to talk to people, after so many years of being silent."

Juliet stared up at the Sixth Earl of Cross's cruel face, her chest throbbing with such a deep pain it felt as if her heart was breaking in two, yet at the same time her mind was racing, snatching at those fragments of memories of the time she'd spent with Miles in London.

He'd talked to her, then. Oh, it had taken a great deal of teasing and chattering at him to peel back his layers, but once she'd broken through that hard, thick shell she'd found a funny, tender, and caring man hidden underneath.

A man she'd thought she could love.

"It doesn't help that Cross is so frighteningly intelligent. He scares the wits out of most people, and so they give him a wide berth." Lord Barnaby studied her for a moment. "Not you, though, Miss Templeton. You don't seem to be afraid of him in the least."

"No, but I'm a scandalous lady from a scandalous family, my lord. It's easy enough to be bold when you haven't anything to lose." She'd had her own challenges, of course, but she'd also had the comfort of a warm, loving family. She knew what love was, how much it meant, and that was far more than Miles had ever known.

"I think it's likely Cross will retire from society once this house party ends. I've always wanted better for him, and hoped he'd find his way to happiness somehow, but he's the stubbornest man alive, and won't listen to reason."

She whirled toward him, a sudden roaring in her ears, and her heart crashing hard against her ribs. "What do you mean?"

"I doubt he'll spend much time in London in the future, if any. I know my cousin, Miss Templeton. He'll bury himself up in this dismal place, and remain here alone for the rest of his days. Steeple Cross is farther from London, and much more isolated than his seat in Kent—"

"Here? You think he intends to stay *here*?" This godforsaken place, with its endless gray skies and torrential rains? It's horrible, claw-footed furniture, and dreary, dark paneling everywhere? "But a man doesn't just drop out of sight, my lord! Why, I've never heard of such a—"

She broke off with a gasp, her heart plummeting. She *had* heard of such a thing, had watched a once confident, vigorous man withdraw from society, had witnessed him fade by degrees, one month after the next until there'd been nothing left of him but a handful of dust.

That man had been her father.

After their mother's scandal she'd abandoned them all, and he... he'd never left Hambleden House again, once she'd gone.

He'd *died* there.

Lord Barnaby was shaking his head. "I daresay he's already made up his mind, Miss Templeton."

"But... but he can't!" It was an absurd thing to say, because of course, he could. He was an earl. He could do whatever he pleased, even something destined to render the rest of his life as lonely as the start had been.

"Why else would he be so determined to see me wed? One of us must marry and produce an heir, and he's made up his mind it won't be him. Cross may not understand love, but he understands duty." Lord Barnaby's laugh was bitter. "His father made certain of that."

"He's returning to the life that made him so miserable as a child? Willingly?" She seized Lord Barnaby's coat sleeve. "You mustn't let him, my lord! You have to talk to him, make him see reason!"

What would become of him, if he remained at Steeple Cross alone? What sort of life could he hope to have, in this cold, empty place?

A short one, and a dreadfully lonely one.

"I've tried, but you'll never find a more obstinate man than Cross, and... Miss Templeton? Where are you going?"

"Why, to talk some sense into your ridiculous cousin, of course!" She had a great deal of experience scolding obstinate sisters, and earl or not, Miles was only one man, and thus no match for a lady of her skills. "Where is he?"

"Still in his study, I'd wager, frowning at the fire and cradling his bottle of port."

She snatched her skirts up and hurried toward the stairs, the hollow thud of her shoes against the wooden floor echoing in the cavernous space.

Lord Barnaby followed her down the paneled corridor, calling out advice as she rushed down the stairs —something about not paying any mind when Cross behaved like an arrogant aristocrat, and warning her not to mention embroidered waistcoats, of all things, because they put Cross in a temper, and reminding her his cousin was dreadfully mulish, and would do everything he could not to listen to her.

But he *would* listen to her.

She wouldn't give him any other choice.

CHAPTER
FOURTEEN

When his study door flew open an hour later, Miles's first thought was it must be Barnaby. His cousin had been rushing madly through every door he encountered since he was a child, and had never reconciled himself to entering a room with the dignity that befitted a nobleman.

But it wasn't Barnaby. It was Juliet, panting, her hair coming loose, and a handful of wrinkled skirts clutched in her fist, as if she'd been running.

He leapt to his feet, the edge of his boot knocking against the empty bottle of port he'd left on the floor, sending it rolling across the carpet. "Juliet! What is it?" Was she trying to escape Boggs? "If Lord Boggs has forgotten himself so thoroughly as to—"

"No, I... no. I was in a hurry so I would catch you before you retired for the evening."

She was rushing about like a pack of hounds were at her heels so she might see *him*? That was... not at all remarkable, or even interesting. There was no reason for his heart to attempt a leap from his chest, so he yanked it back down again, like tugging the string of a kite soaring through the sky.

No good ever came of soaring, as it ended, inevitably, with *landing*. "You've caught me, Miss Templeton. May I offer you some sherry? I'm afraid the carpet has finished off the port."

She let out a nervous laugh. "Oh, no thank you, my lord, I just... I wondered if I might have a quick word with you."

"Of course." He gestured her to the chair beside his, but once she was seated, she remained silent, staring at him with a troubled expression until he cleared his throat. "It must be a matter of some importance, as I've never known you to be at a loss for words before."

Her lips twitched. "Well, I'll own it's rather unusual."

"Unheard of, even," he murmured, teasing her.

"Why, what an unfair exaggeration, Lord Cross. You sound very much like my sisters."

"Well, you *did* say they were all clever."

She laughed. "Oh, yes, very clever, but none of us ever learned how to preserve a ladylike silence."

"Nor should you. A lady of such charm and wit should never be silent."

God knew he didn't have any patience for silly chits who nattered endlessly at him, but Juliet was one of only a few ladies whose conversation made her *more* attractive to him, rather than less so. He'd admired her from the first—he was a man, after all, and she was exquisite, her blue eyes alone enough to warm even the coldest of hearts—but lovely faces were as common as white cravats in London.

Such a sly wit, though, falling from such dainty, ladylike lips?

That was unexpected, and it knocked him off guard just long enough for her to slip past his careful defenses. She'd been wreaking havoc on him ever since, quickening his breath, and making him ache with longing.

"My goodness." A delicate pink blush rose to her cheeks. "You're very gallant this evening, my lord."

"It's not gallantry, Juliet. It's merely the truth."

Her eyes met his, the deep, dark blue of heavens and oceans, and the air between them swelled with awareness, the low buzz of it in his ears, the pulse of it low in his belly. They gazed at each other in silence, until her lips parted, and he realized he'd been staring at them.

His heart was pounding, thundering in his ears, everything inside him giving way to the hot rush of blood in his veins, and it was some moments before he could make sense of what she was saying.

"... tell you about my father."

"Your father?" She'd come bursting into his study at this hour, to tell him about her father? "I don't understand. I wasn't acquainted with him."

"No, but you've heard of my family's misfortunes, my lord, along with the rest of London."

"Your mother's scandal? Yes, I heard of it." It had been several years since her mother had fled London with her aristocratic lover, yet the *ton* wouldn't let it go. They still spoke of it with such malicious delight, it was as if it had just happened.

"I believe the *ton* refers to it as my mother's scandal, yes, though it was never hers as much as it was *ours*, as we were the ones left to face the consequences of it. Scandal is inconvenient that way, isn't it? Rather like smallpox. It leaves its marks on everyone unfortunate enough to cross its path."

There was a bleakness in her voice utterly at odds with everything he knew about her. "It pains you to speak of it."

"Yes."

"Then you needn't tell me—"

"I want to tell you, my lord. Not the salacious bits the *ton* salivates over, but about what happened after she'd gone. The *ton* never bothers much with that. No doubt they think it as dull as a church sermon."

Dull? No, it wouldn't be that. Heartbreaking, yes, enough so that the selfish part of him didn't want to hear her speak of it, but if she could bear to say it aloud, then he could bear to listen to her. "Very well, if you wish."

"Thank you, my lord." She was quiet for a moment, her gaze on the fire, but when she turned to face him, she was determined. "It was dreadful, of course. Far worse in the aftermath than in the moment. It's astonishing, really, how quickly everything fell apart, as if we'd been balanced on the head of a pin our entire lives, only waiting to topple over."

"Lives are fragile things, aren't they?" Like a fire that burned brightly, but extinguished itself quickly.

"More so than I'd realized, yes. My eldest sister Euphemia was betrothed at the time, but the scandal put a rather brutal end to it. She's never been the same since, and I doubt she ever will be."

"Her betrothed was a villain then, and a coward." He'd never before laid eyes on Euphemia Templeton, yet he was, somehow, choking with fury on her behalf.

"He was in no way worthy of Euphemia's heart. As for Emmeline... well, you know her yourself, so I'll only say she so dreads another scandal she's considering refusing Lord Melrose's hand in a desperate attempt to avoid a second one."

"She won't actually refuse him, surely?"

"I can't be certain, but she may, yes. Pure folly, given she's quite irrevocably in love with him, and pointless, as well, for it won't do any good. Scandal will come either way."

"Yes." It would come—*had* come—and was devouring everything in its path. Any attempt to stop it now would be as futile as trying to put his spilled port back in the bottle.

"As for Helena and Tilly, the two youngest, they escaped relatively unscathed, as they were too young at the time to be much affected by it."

"Small mercies."

"Disappointingly small, yes." She paused. "You're aware, my lord, that my father died last year?"

Her tone shifted when she mentioned her father, as if she were handling a thing with jagged edges that would cut her if she didn't take the utmost care with it. "I am, yes."

"The *ton* believes my mother's scandal and abandonment are to blame for his death. Their opinions mean nothing to me, but my sisters think so, too."

"You don't think so?"

"No. He loved her, and he was devastated by her betrayal. I don't deny it precipitated his decline, but it wasn't what caused his death. He died because he gave up, my lord."

"What did he give up, Juliet?" But he already

knew. James Templeton had become a recluse after his wife's disgrace.

"Everything. He cast all his friends aside, and fled London for our home in Buckinghamshire. He confined himself to our property, at first, but over time, he grew increasingly reluctant to leave Hambleden House itself. By the time he died, it had been six months since he'd set foot outdoors."

Ah, so that's what this was. Her sudden appearance in his study, her strange insistence on discussing her father...this was a cautionary tale, a warning not to let the same thing happen to him. "You've been speaking with Lord Barnaby, haven't you?"

"Your cousin is concerned for you, Lord Cross. He's afraid you'll be unhappy if you remain at Steeple Cross alone."

"Alone, with two dozen servants, Miss Templeton? Lord Barnaby has exaggerated the situation. He has visions of me barring the front door and retreating to my study, never to emerge again, but I can assure you I don't intend to become a recluse."

What was the word Barnaby had used? Hermit.

"No one *intend*s to become a recluse, my lord." She gave him a sad smile. "It happens by degrees, and so gradually one doesn't notice it until it's too late."

"It won't happen to *me*."

He wouldn't venture back into town anytime soon, but that was nothing new. He'd always despised town, and avoided it as much as possible. He didn't intend to entertain, either, but he'd see Barnaby and Lady Cora, and Melrose, of course.

When the weather permitted it. Steeple Cross was rather isolated, and the Oxfordshire weather could be harsh, with snow and ice rendering the roads impassable.

But that was only during the winter months—

"You can't imagine how painful it is to watch a loved one deteriorate as my father did, Lord Cross." Her voice was soft. "To see him so broken, such a pale shadow of his former self. People aren't meant to be alone, to be cut off from everyone who—"

"*Which* people, Juliet?"

She jumped, her eyes going wide.

Damn it, he hadn't meant to raise his voice to her, but with every word she said the hard, tight knot in his chest pulled tighter, and he couldn't bear to hear any more. "I beg your pardon. I'm sorry for your family, but what was true for your father might not be true for another man."

"I don't understand. What do you mean?"

"I mean that some people *are* meant to be alone." His father, for one.

"What are you saying, my lord?" She paused, her throat working. "Do you mean you consider *yourself* to be one of those people?"

Did he? He'd been certain of it, once, but it was no longer as black and white as it had been. Perhaps Barnaby was right, and he wasn't as much like his father as he'd always supposed, but what if...

What if Barnaby was wrong? What if he gave in to the demands of his heart, and brought Juliet to Steeple Cross, or to his seat in Kent, and it turned out Barnaby was *wrong*? That he *was* the sort of man who ruined people, just like his father had been?

"Yes. I've never liked people much." And for the most part, they'd returned the favor. "I'm not a tolerant man, Juliet, nor a particularly kind one."

A heavy silence fell between them then, stretching until it had pulled into a fine, gossamer thread, but like a spiderweb, it refused to snap. It kept pulling tighter, thinner, taking his nerves with it until they were screaming in protest.

"Is that what you think?" She whispered at last.

He swallowed, shrugged.

"Then you don't see yourself as I see you." She rose to her feet, and made her way to the door. "I see you, Miles. I have from the start."

He should let her go—let her walk out, and put an end to this agony, but...

Not yet. *Not yet.* "Wait, Juliet."

She paused at the door, her back to him still.

Don't touch her...

But it was too late. He was already reaching for her, turning her to face him, his fingers sliding under her chin, tipping her face up to his. The study was dark, but the footmen had lit the lamps in the hallway, and the light caught the curve of her cheekbone, her shadowed blue eyes.

"What of *you*, Juliet? You never said how your family's scandal affected you."

Her lips curved in something that wasn't a smile. "I was a romantic child, Lord Cross, and when I grew older, I became a silly, starry-eyed, romantic young lady with foolish notions about love righting every wrong, and triumphing over every adversary, but it's more of a struggle now, to retain my faith in love."

It was, somehow, the worst thing she could have said, and he caught his breath as pain seared through him. "But you haven't utterly lost faith, have you? You still think love can triumph, don't you?"

Why did it matter to him? He'd long since given

up whatever faith he'd had in love, if he'd ever had any to begin with. What difference did it make if she had, as well?

Yet he was holding his breath, waiting for her answer.

"I think... I think you were right all along, Lord Cross."

He didn't *want* to be right, not about any of this. "I was right about what?"

She caught his wrist and, as gentle as a whisper, drew his hand away from her face. "*Romeo and Juliet* isn't a romance. It's never been anything but a tragedy."

And with that she was gone, melting into the shadows as if she'd never been there at all.

CHAPTER
FIFTEEN

Juliet passed silently through the entryway, her hems whisking over the checkered marble floor, the muted tap of her slippers louder than they should be as she mounted the stairs, one slow step at a time.

She'd tried her best, and it hadn't done the least bit of good.

Tap.

Of course, it hadn't. How could she have believed a few words from her would somehow undo the damage a lifetime of paternal slights, misjudgments, and cruelties had done to Miles? She, who was even now sinking under the weight of her own mother's betrayal, despite all her flailing and thrashing to keep her head above water?

Tap.

It didn't matter that every word she said to him had been the simple truth. Emmeline was right. The truth had much less power than a persuasive lie, especially the lies one believed about themselves.

That he was cold and unkind, and deserved to be

alone. That he could isolate himself, and the worst wouldn't happen to him, or to those he loved.

That loneliness wouldn't break his heart.

He *wasn't* charming, no. Indeed, he was surly and impatient, with a sharp tongue and an even sharper glare, and forthright to the point of arrogance.

Tap.

Why, she'd never encountered a *less* charming man in her life.

Or a more loyal man, or a better friend, or one more determined that his cousin be happy. Or a kinder one, though he took pains to hide it under a prickly layer of barbs.

A man with the handsomest dark eyes she'd ever seen—

"Ah, here you are at last, Miss Templeton."

She whirled around, her hand flying to her chest. "Oh! Lord Boggs! My goodness, where did you come from?" What in the world was he doing, lurking in the shadows like that? He'd nearly sent her toppling down the stairs!

"I'm not a patient man, Miss Templeton, and you've kept me waiting for some time tonight." He caught her arm, his grip tight.

"I beg your pardon? I hadn't the faintest idea you were waiting for me, my lord." Nor did she see any reason why he should be. She cast a pointed glare at his hand, but instead of releasing her, he pulled her closer.

"Come now, Miss Templeton, don't be coy. You must be aware I came here for you, and quite a lot of bother it's caused me, too."

"I'm sorry for your trouble, my lord, but despite what you told Lord Barnaby, I didn't either ask or expect you to come here, nor was I in any great need of your company."

It was as crushing a speech as she'd ever dared deliver, but he only laughed. "Well, you can't suppose I came all the way to Oxfordshire for Cross's company, eh? No, indeed. It's time you and I discuss the unfinished business between us, and come to an understanding."

"Forgive me, my lord, but I don't know what you're talking about." Nor did she choose to discuss whatever it was *now*, in a darkened stairway at midnight, without another soul in sight.

"No? That *is* a great pity, my dear, but I'm rather, ah... eager to come to an agreement. I thought I'd been plain regarding my intentions toward you, but you slipped through my fingers before I could declare myself, you wicked girl."

Wicked girl? For pity's sake. "I don't have the pleasure of understanding you, Lord Boggs."

"I think you understand me very well, Miss Templeton. I've been enamored of you from the moment I laid eyes on you, and I wish to make you mine."

His? Dear God, what an appalling thought.

Yet, was she really in any position to scorn such an offer? If Lord Melrose was back in London, as Lord Boggs claimed he was, Emmeline may have already refused him. If so, then her family's situation remained as dire as it had been before she and Emmeline ventured to London for the season. Worse, in fact, now they had a fresh scandal hanging over their heads.

All their worries would vanish if she made such an advantageous marriage.

Lord Boggs, though! She didn't love him, would

never love him, and despite his flowery speech about being enamored of her, he didn't love her, either.

A marriage between them would be... how had Miles once put it?

An exchange of favors.

She wished to save her family from destitution, and he wanted a young bride with a pretty face to wear on his arm—a mere trinket, nothing more—and a marriage between them would mean a lifetime of being at the mercy of his every whim.

The very idea made a shudder of revulsion dart up her spine, but since her father's death, her life was no longer about what she *wanted*. Helena had already gone out to work. Soon enough, they'd all be obliged to go into service. They'd lose Hambleden House, and would only rarely see each other then.

Wasn't it time she gave up the girlish hopes she'd been foolish enough to cherish at one time? She was no longer a child, and this wasn't a romantic novel destined for a happy ending.

Yet it wasn't a tragedy, either.

She squared her shoulders, and met his smug gaze. "I thank you most sincerely for the great honor you do me, my lord, but I cannot accept—"

"Honor?" He stared at her, then threw his head back in a laugh. "Oh no, my dear! I'm afraid you've misunderstood me. A marriage between us is quite out of the question. Your scandal put an end to any plans I may have had of making you a countess. No, I've another arrangement in mind."

Arrangement? What did he mean, an *arrangement*? What other arrangement was there, aside from—

Oh, dear God. Dear *God*, was he asking her to become his *mistress?*

"Need I remind you of your pitiable circumstances, my dear? Your family is a scandal, your coffers are empty, and your reputation is in tatters. Melrose isn't going to save you, and you have nothing but your pretty face to fall back on. I'm prepared to be quite generous if you please me, so think carefully before you refuse my—"

"How *dare* you?"

She didn't *plan* it, or even realize she'd done it until his head snapped back, and then her palm was stinging like it had caught fire, and his face was turning red, then redder still—

"How dare *I?*" He seized her arm, a curse on his lips, and jerked it behind her back. "You're a bloody little tease."

"Release me this in—"

"You've been tormenting me for *weeks.*" He wrenched her closer, his fingers biting into her flesh. "You're a slippery little bit, but I have you now." His face was a mere inch from hers, the stench of cigars and port on his breath. "Now be a good girl, and do as I say."

He wrenched her off her feet as if she weighed no more than a feather, the toes of her slippers dragging silently over the thick carpet as he pulled her from the landing into the dark hallway beyond.

"Let go!" A scream was building in her throat, but before she could give it voice, he slapped a hand over her mouth. "Quiet," he hissed, his other hand fumbling with her bodice.

Her stomach lurched, and bile flooded her throat, hot and acrid, choking her, and she couldn't breathe... she couldn't *breathe*—

"*Umph*." There was a gasp or a grunt, low and pained in her ear, and in the next breath the grabbing hands were gone, and she was swaying on shaking legs in the middle of the dim hallway, and Lord Boggs was at her feet, doubled over and holding his stomach.

She didn't pause, and she didn't look back, but fled down the hallway, clutching the gaping neck of her gown in her fist. A sob rose in her chest and burned up her throat, but she choked it back and stumbled on, around corners and down hallways she'd never seen, past doorways she didn't recognize.

She ran until she was panting, her heart thrashing in her chest, turning one corner after another, certain she heard the thud of heavy footsteps behind her. When she stopped at last her hair was tumbling down her back, her eyes were blurry with tears, and she was lost in some corridor in Steeple Cross she'd never set foot in before.

Thud.

She froze as the muffled footsteps came toward her. It was Lord Boggs, come after her! It must be. She pressed flat against the wall behind her, gasping for breath, her heart shuddering with panic, but there was no place to hide, and his footsteps were drawing closer—

"Miss Templeton? Are you lost, miss?"

"Sarah." Juliet sagged against the wall, weak-kneed with relief. "I, ah... it's the silliest thing, but I'm afraid I got turned around on my way back to my bedchamber."

As lies went, it was a pitiful one, but it was all she could do not to burst into tears.

Sarah wasn't fooled, of course. Her kind brown

eyes widened as she took in Juliet's disheveled hair and clothing, but she didn't ask any questions, bless her. "It happens all the time, miss. Steeple Cross is a big, confusing place."

"It is, isn't it?" In more ways than one.

"Shall I just fasten your buttons for you, miss?" Sarah didn't wait for an answer, but set the heavy coal scuttle she was carrying down on the floor, turned Juliet gently around and fastened the row of buttons on the back of her gown. Then with a few quick tugs, she settled her skirts in place. "There you are, miss. That's much better."

"Thank you, Sarah." Tears were threatening again, her nose burning and her throat aching, but she held them back with ruthless determination. At the very least, she could do her best not to fall utterly to pieces in front of poor Sarah. "If you could point me in the direction of my bedchamber, Sarah, I'd be most grateful to you."

"I'll take you there myself, miss." Sarah gave her a reassuring smile. "I was just going to the guest wing to see to the fires, in any case."

"How fortunate. Thank you." Juliet followed after her like a lost puppy, down one corridor after the next, around a dozen corners and past endless closed doors, until at last they turned into the hallway with the familiar green-and-gold patterned carpet, and the green-striped wallpaper.

"Here you are, Miss Templeton. Shall I come lay a fire for—"

"No, thank you, Sarah." She wouldn't be here long enough to enjoy a fire. "I'll be fine. You're very kind. Thank you."

"Of course, miss." There was unmistakable sympathy in Sarah's eyes, but she only nodded again, and made her way down the corridor, back in the direction they'd come.

Juliet hurried into her bedchamber, closed the door behind her and fell back against it, her breath hitching. The urge to throw herself onto her bed and succumb to a despairing flood of tears was unbearable, but there wasn't time.

She'd have to move quickly.

She peeled her eyelids up from sticky, aching eyes and glanced at the door that connected her room to Lady Fosberry's. If she opened that door right now, woke Lady Fosberry and poured all her misery out at her ladyship's feet, Lady Fosberry would soothe and pet and reassure her, and then she'd do whatever Juliet asked of her, even if it meant a hasty retreat from Steeple Cross.

The two of them could be tucked into a carriage and on the road back to London within the hour. But Lady Fosberry was no fool, nor was she naïve. She'd see at once that something had gone terribly amiss, and she wouldn't rest until she found out what it was.

Once she did...

She'd never allow her dear young friend to be so grievously insulted without doing everything in her power to see it set to rights, and then there'd be no end to this miserable business.

No. She couldn't bear it. It turned her stomach.

So, she didn't approach the connecting door. Instead, she hurried to the desk, fumbled about until she found paper, a pen and some ink, and scrawled a hasty note to her ladyship. Then she changed into her warmest traveling dress, donned her cloak, stuffed a few bits and pieces she thought she'd need into her valise, and pushed the note under the connecting door.

Then she slipped out, and took care to pay attention to where she was going.

"Juliet? My goodness, you're up early." Lady Cora was still rubbing the sleep from her eyes when she opened her bedchamber door.

"Yes, I beg your pardon for waking you. I need..." She needed so many things, she hardly knew where to begin.

But what she needed most was to leave Steeple Cross. *Now.*

"Dear me, you're already dressed. You make me feel quite lazy. Where are you going at such an early..." Lady Cora trailed off, her smile fading when she noticed Juliet's expression. "Oh, dear. Something dreadful has happened, hasn't it?"

"I'm afraid so, yes, but there's no time for me to tell you now." Lady Cora would hear of it soon enough, just as everyone else at Steeple Cross would. "But I need a favor, Cora. Will you help me?"

Lady Cora's pretty blue eyes went wide, but she didn't hesitate. "Of course, I will. Anything."

Dear, sweet Lady Cora. Befriending her was the one thing she'd done right since she'd come to Steeple Cross, the one thing she could never regret. Tears threatened again, but Juliet swallowed them back, *again*. When she allowed herself to shed them at last, they'd likely drown her.

"May I have your permission to ask your coachman to take me in your carriage to Lord Hawke's estate this morning? It's only about eight miles from here, so I daresay he'll be back before anyone awakens. My younger sister Helena is governess there, and I—I must see her at once."

A dozen different questions flashed in Lady Cora's eyes, but bless her, she didn't ask a single one. "Of course, you may. Let me dress quickly, and I'll come down with you."

"No. It's all right." She didn't want Lady Cora involved in this awful business. "I'll find him myself. Thank you, Cora."

She pressed a quick kiss to her friend's cheek, then turned and ran down the hallway toward the stairs. There was no one about, either on the stairway or in the entryway, so she tiptoed down the stairs, glancing nervously over her shoulder as she went, and made her way down the corridor that led to Miles's study.

The door was closed.

She passed by it without pausing, and slipped into the library.

It was deserted, thankfully. She had one final thing to do before she left Steeple Cross, and she'd rather no one was about to see her do it.

She closed the door behind her, then crossed the room to the bookshelves that held Miles's large collection of plays. She reached over her head, pulled down *Romeo and Juliet*, slid a folded piece of paper between its pages, then replaced the volume on the shelf.

Perhaps he'd find it someday, and he'd understand what she'd been trying to tell him last night. She wouldn't be here to see it, but that didn't matter.

It mattered only that he knew.

CHAPTER

SIXTEEN

T he next morning Miles awoke from a fitful sleep feeling very much like a man who'd spent half of the previous evening drowning himself in a bottle of port, and the other half drowning in doubts.

His head was heavy, his eyes gritty, and his stomach sloshing with a nauseating combination of undigested port and uneasiness. It hadn't been an enjoyable evening. He'd argued with his cousin, then he'd argued with Juliet, then he'd buried his fist in Lord Boggs's eye socket.

Or had he only dreamed that last part?

"Good morning, Lord Cross." Vincent, his valet, was bustling around the bedchamber, fussing and straightening.

"Why are you here so early, Vincent?"

"I beg your pardon, my lord, but it's eight o'clock, my usual time."

That late? He rose up onto one elbow, blinking the sleep from his eyes. His bedchamber was much lighter than usual, the sun several hours past the horizon.

"Will you have the dark gray coat today, my lord, or the dark blue?" Vincent turned from the wardrobe, a coat in each hand.

Miles squinted at them. "They look exactly the same."

Vincent blinked, then returned the navy coat to the wardrobe. "The dark gray, then."

Miles ran a weary hand through his hair, and fell back against the bed. "Do you know if I happened to assault Lord Boggs last night, Vincent?"

Vincent had set the gray coat aside for brushing, and was busily arranging Miles's shaving things on a clean towel, but now he looked up, eyebrows raised. "No, my lord, not that I'm aware of."

Damn it. It had been the only enjoyable part of the entire evening. "Pity. Someone should."

"Are you unwell, my lord?" Vincent abandoned the shaving implements and hurried to the foot of the bed to peer closely at Miles. "It's unlike you to, er... threaten your house guests."

He *wasn't* well. Far from it. Nor would he be, until he spoke to Juliet.

He swung his legs over the side of the bed, found last night's breeches in a tangle on the floor and pulled them up over his hips.

"My lord?" Vincent was gaping at him, scandalized. "I've got fresh breeches for you right here. I've just pressed—"

"Never mind the breeches, Vincent, and don't bother with the coat, either. Just fetch me a shirt, will you?"

Vincent rushed to do his bidding, letting out a choked sound when Miles only paused long enough to don the shirt, fasten his breeches and stuff his feet into his boots. "You're not going out like that, my lord? That is, I beg your pardon, Lord Cross, but—"

"You can pretty me up later, Vincent. I've some urgent business to attend to first."

Juliet may still be in the breakfast parlor. He'd start there, and work his way up until he found her, and if he had to chase her all over the house like a lovestruck schoolboy, then so be it.

But she wasn't in the breakfast parlor. It was deserted, aside from Lady Drummond, who was sitting at the table with an untouched plate of food in front of her, reading a letter. "Good morning, Lady Drummond."

She looked up, a troubled frown on her brow. "Oh, Lord Cross. I beg your pardon. I didn't hear you come in. Good morning."

"Is something amiss?" Judging by Lady Drummond's expression, it was either that, or the cream had gone off.

"I'm... not sure. The post road from Chipping Norton has been flooded for days now, but they've at last got it clear, so your servant was able to fetch the post this morning. I've had a letter from my sister."

"I trust she's well?" He hoped so, because he couldn't stand a long recitation of Lady Drummond's sister's ailments right now.

"Yes, thank you, very well, but she says something strange." She nodded at her letter. "Were you aware, my lord, that Lord Boggs is recently betrothed?"

"Betrothed." That couldn't be right. "Are you certain, Lady Drummond?"

"Yes. My sister says he's betrothed to Lady Louisa Montagu."

If Boggs was betrothed, then what was he doing

at Steeple Cross, prowling after Juliet? It didn't make sense, unless—

That bloody *blackguard*.

"It's rather worrying, really, that Lord Boggs should be paying such marked attention to Miss Templeton, if he's betrothed."

Damnation. He should have blacked both Boggs's eyes while he slept last night.

"You don't think that Lord Boggs..." Lady Drummond trailed off, her cheeks coloring.

That Boggs came to Steeple Cross with dishonorable intentions toward Juliet? That was *precisely* what he thought. "I think, Lady Drummond, that I must have a word with Lord Boggs."

"Oh, dear." The letter fell from Lady Drummond's fingers and drifted to the table. "Lady Fosberry is going to be dreadfully upset."

Upset? No. Lady Fosberry would be apoplectic. "If you'll pardon me, Lady Drummond, I'll go see to Lord Boggs at once."

Every inch of him was quivering with rage as he mounted the stairs, and when he turned down the corridor to the guest wing and saw Boggs standing outside Juliet's bedchamber door, it the simmer sparked into an inferno.

He froze a half a dozen steps away from Boggs, breathing hard as he struggled to control the wrath blazing him. If he got too close to the man now, he'd tear his head off.

"Morning, Cross. Have you seen Miss Templeton?"

"I beg your pardon?" A more perceptive man than Boggs may have noticed the cold edge to his voice, the stillness of a body on the verge of exploding into violence, but Boggs didn't realize his danger yet, and merely rolled his eyes.

"Miss *Templeton*, Cross. I'm on the hunt for Miss Templeton. Have you seen her yet this morning?"

"What do you want with Miss Templeton, Boggs?" He knew, of course, he knew, but he wanted to hear Boggs say it aloud, so he'd have no reason to reproach himself for what he was going to do to the villain.

"The same thing any man would want with Miss Templeton, eh, Cross?" Boggs gave him a conspiratorial smirk, as if the two of them shared some sort of amusing joke.

Miles closed in on him, hands flexing at his sides. "I don't have the pleasure of understanding you. Perhaps you'd care to explain what you mean."

"Come now, Cross. You're not blind, and she's a tempting little bit. I don't want to let her slip through my fingers, unless... is she yours?"

Miles's lips, his jaw, even his teeth had gone as tight as a drum. "*Mine*?"

"By God, Cross, you're a sly one. You've rather ruined my plans for her, but there are dozens of other pretty little birds of paradise to be had in London, eh? Perhaps I'll have another go at her, once you've finished with her."

Miles advanced on Boggs with his fists so tightly clenched the skin over his knuckles threatened to tear. "Do you dare impugn the lady's honor, Boggs?"

His voice was dangerously soft, a low, threatening hiss, and at last Boggs realized he'd made a drastic error in judgement. "I—well no, of course not, I just... I beg your pardon, Cross. I didn't realize you'd gotten there first, or else I would never—"

Boggs got no further, because Miles seized him by the throat and slammed him up against the wall. "Not *another word*. If you *ever* dare to speak her name again, you'll be calling your seconds, and meeting me at dawn."

Boggs's eyes bulged, the color leaching from his face. "T-there's no need for that, Cross. Why, that business last night was nothing, nothing at all. I hardly laid a finger—"

"You *touched* her?" He wrenched Boggs away from the wall, then slammed him back into it again with enough force the doors around them rattled.

There was a thump, and an instant later, Lady Fosberry threw open the door to Juliet's bedchamber. She didn't say a word, only stared at Boggs with such disgust that even he, a man with no shame or scruples, cringed and swallowed.

If Boggs could swallow, then Miles's fingers weren't bloody tight enough, so he squeezed until Boggs's face turned a mottled shade of purple.

"I swear I never t-touched her, Cross! Never! I-I, oh, no! I, er, I meant to say I—"

Slam. "You're a bloody liar. See to your seconds, Boggs—"

"Lord Cross!" Lady Fosberry raised her voice to a shout to be heard over Boggs's whimpering and sniveling. "There will be no duels. I absolutely *forbid* it. You do Juliet no favors with such behavior!"

Miles hesitated. He'd love nothing more than to spill Boggs's blood, but as badly as he ached to bury a ball in his flesh, Lady Fosberry was right. A duel between them would hurt Juliet, and he wouldn't allow her to be hurt ever again.

Not by anyone, least of all himself.

He loved her more than he hated Boggs.

So, he did as Lady Fosberry bid, and flung Boggs away from him. "You have Lady Fosberry to thank for saving your miserable skin, but if I ever hear even a *breath* of gossip about Miss Templeton, I'll come for you, and you'll find yourself at the other end of my pistol."

"Not a word, Lord Cross, I swear it! N-not a single word. Indeed, I've always admired Miss Templeton, truly, and would never dream of insulting—"

"Get out of my house. *Now*."

"Yes, yes, of course, at once!" Boggs continued to babble as he backed down the corridor, then scurried around the corner like a fleeing rat.

"Well, Lord Cross." Lady Fosberry crossed her arms over her chest. "That was quite a performance."

Miles was still panting with rage. "You should have let me shoot him."

Her lips pursed with disapproval. "Forgive me, my lord, but I think a screaming brawl in the hallway is quite enough for one morning."

"Where is Juliet?" He looked past Lady Fosberry into Juliet's bedchamber, but it was empty.

"Gone."

"Gone," he repeated dumbly. "Where?"

"She left very early this morning in Lady Drummond's carriage. She's at Lord Hawke's estate in Charlbury with her sister, Helena. Here." She thrust a letter at him, then waited while he read it. "Now then, Lord Cross, may I assume by that woebegone expression on your face that you've come to your senses regarding Juliet, at last?"

He'd either come to his senses, or lost them entirely. He hardly knew which. The only thing he was certain of was that he was desperately in love with Juliet Templeton, and every moment that passed without her knowing it was pure torture. "Yes, my lady."

Her forbidding expression softened. "Good. I suppose you'd better go and fetch her, then, but not just yet. Let her have a day alone with her sister before you go racing off to Hawke's Run. Helena Templeton is wise beyond her years, and will set Juliet back to rights. She'll be more willing to listen to you then."

Pure torture, then, but perhaps he deserved it.

He made his way back to his bedchamber to find Vincent waiting for him. "Lord Cross, here you are. I've got your gray coat and black waistcoat right—"

"No. Not the black, Vincent. I want the scarlet today."

Vincent sucked in a breath. "The *scarlet*? You mean the—"

"Yes. The scarlet waistcoat with the gold embroidered suns." For what he had in mind, only the scarlet waistcoat would do.

Vincent had gone white. "Yes, I... yes, of course, but... oh, dear. What does one wear with a scarlet waistcoat, my lord? Shall I fetch the gray coat? Or perhaps the blue would be—"

"No coat, Vincent."

"No coat," Vincent echoed faintly. "Yes, my lord."

Vincent fussed and tugged him into respectably drab navy breeches, and only whimpered a little as he helped Miles into the scarlet waistcoat. "Well done, Vincent. Perhaps you'd better have a little lie-down now."

"Yes, I... I think I shall, my lord."

He left Vincent in a half swoon, and made his way downstairs to the library.

He'd promised Lady Fosberry he wouldn't go to Juliet at once, but he could put the time until then to good use.

The volume was sitting in its place on the bookshelf where they'd left it the day before. He took it down, but as he was turning to the door to retreat to the privacy of his study, a folded paper fell out from between the pages, and fluttered to the window seat.

Juliet's sketch. He recognized it at once.

He'd made an almighty fuss over that sketch, demanding to see it, then he'd forgotten it completely the instant his lips met hers.

But *she* hadn't forgotten.

He unfolded the paper, then dropped onto the window seat and sat there while the clock ticked off the silent minutes, staring at it.

She drew with a confident hand—loose, fluid pencil lines and delicate shading, a little rough in places, and a little disproportionate in others, but...

It was him.

He traced a finger over the chin and jaw, both angular and firm, but not hard or cruel, as he'd always thought them. His lips were fuller, too, with just the barest hint of a smile at one corner, and his eyes... they weren't watchful or cold at all. Serious, yes, but with a certain softness to them, even a kindness, within a frame of long dark lashes.

This wasn't the haughty, ill-tempered, arrogant Earl of Cross. Not the frigid, unfeeling man who'd brought more than one young lady to tears with a single cutting glance, or the arrogant nobleman whose mind, tongue, and heart were edged in steel.

His father had been that sort of man. He'd offended people, dismissed them, and he'd done it deliberately. He'd understood the difference between kindness and cruelty. He'd chosen cruelty, because he simply didn't care whom he hurt.

But Miles *did* care. He'd just never known how to behave in a way that showed it.

But he wasn't his father. At least, he didn't have to be.

I see you, Miles. I have from the start.

And she had. She'd seen what nearly everyone else had failed to see.

What *he'd* failed to see.

He gazed down at the man in the drawing, this man who was him, yet was unfamiliar to him at the same time.

Couldn't Juliet fall in love with *this* man? Want *him*?

He picked up the drawing, folded it carefully, and slipped it into his waistcoat pocket. Then he took up the book—*Romeo and Juliet*, of course—and left the library for his study.

And there, with his heart in his throat and a whispered prayer on his lips, he began to read.

CHAPTER
SEVENTEEN

Juliet stared listlessly out of the carriage window as she and Lady Drummond's coachman made their way across the rain-washed countryside that lay between Steeple Cross and the Earl of Hawke's estate, Hawke's Run.

For the first time in seven days, the sun was shining. Well, why shouldn't it? Now she'd been taught her lesson, there was no longer any need for warnings and ill omens, or portents of impending doom. The thought should have comforted her—no more fretting about an angry universe —and no doubt it would comfort her, eventually.

But not yet.

Still, Oxfordshire was beautiful. Now the raging storm had passed, and she no longer felt as if she were perched on the verge of an apocalyptic flood, she could see it was all gentle rolling hills and swathes of verdant green, with picturesque white cottages scattered about that looked like fluffy, low-hanging clouds from a distance.

And sheep, of course. There were always sheep in the English countryside.

It was something, anyway. Perhaps the beauty would comfort Miles in his isolation, unless he went the way of her father, and never again set foot outside the doors of Steeple Cross.

But even that fleeting thought of him made an ominous pressure start to build behind her eyes, so she pushed it aside. It wouldn't do to appear on Helena's doorstep all red-eyed and weepy.

Or, rather, Lord Hawke's doorstep. Dear God, how did she intend to explain her sudden presence to *him*? Helena was his governess, not his countess, and it wasn't the thing for governesses to entertain their family members at their employer's estates.

Perhaps he wasn't at home. She was due for some luck, surely?

As if she'd conjured it into existence from her thoughts, a massive structure of pale gray stone appeared over the next rise. She stared at it through the window, her mouth falling open.

It wasn't a manor house, or one of the usual handsome estates so many aristocratic gentlemen claimed as their country seats. It was... well, there was no other word for it but *castle*. It was a castle, complete with rounded turrets on either end, and chimney stacks rising to such majestic heights it looked as if they were tickling the chin of the sky itself.

Helena had never said a word about *this*, but then it would be like Helena not to have noticed it. The faintest hint of a fond laugh escaped her throat. Oh, it was nothing more than a sickly echo of what it used to be, but it was a relief to discover she was still capable of any sort of laugh, poor, limp thing that it was.

She leaned forward in her seat, nose still pressed to the window, and silently urged the coachman to go faster, to get there sooner. How she'd missed her blunt, practical sister! If anyone could talk some sense into her, it would be Helena.

Oh, why wouldn't the coachman hurry?

At last, he turned onto the long drive that led up to a comparably modest, single-arched doorway, and hurried down from the box to set the step and assist her down.

Before her foot even touched the graveled courtyard, she heard voices. Children's voices, shouting and laughing.

That would be Adrian and Etienne, Helena's charges, the six-year-old twin boys she'd described in her letters. Both of them were terribly naughty—utter savages, or so Helena said—but her tender fondness for them was woven into every line of her letters.

The shouts grew louder, then louder still, the sort of joyful shrieks one only ever heard from energetic children, and a moment later a slender lady with a mop of caramel brown hair darted out from around the side of one of the turrets.

It was Helena, laughing at the two little boys chasing her, their ear-splitting screams threatening to rent a hole in the sky.

"Egads," the coachman muttered. "That's two little imps if I ever saw them." But he was smiling, because it was impossible not to smile in the presence of such wild exuberance. "You're sure you want me to leave you here with them, miss?"

"Oh, yes." She surprised herself by returning his

smile. "My sister is their governess, and she knows how to manage boys."

How Helena had learned that particular skill was a mystery, given there wasn't a single little boy within ten miles of Hambleden House, but there was no time to ponder it. Helena had seen the carriage, and was making her way toward the drive with purposeful steps, her two charges scampering at her heels.

"Right then, miss." The coachman handed her valise to her, then touched his hat and climbed back onto the box.

She gave him a grateful wave, but she hardly noticed as he tapped the horse's backs with the ribbons, and the carriage rattled from the courtyard back down the drive.

Helena's steps had slowed as she drew closer, and now she came to an abrupt stop, her mouth dropping open. "*Juliet?* My goodness, is that *you*?"

She opened her mouth to reply, to tell her sister it was indeed her, but the words froze on her tongue. *Was* it her? She hardly knew. She didn't feel like the same Juliet she'd once been, and this new Juliet was... well, she wasn't an improvement on the old one.

This Juliet was weepy, and morose, and no longer believed in love.

"Why, how wonderful, Juliet!" Helena rushed forward and caught Juliet in her arms. "Where in the world did you come from?"

Juliet let herself sink into her sister's embrace, a foolish, familiar sting pressing behind her eyes. It *was* possible, then, to be in the presence of two adorable and wonderfully naughty little boys, both of whom were now watching her with wide-eyed interest, and not be able to find a smile anywhere inside her.

This time, there was no fighting the hitching in her chest, the burning in her nose. It was coming on like a storm, her eyes growing damp, tears catching in her eyelashes.

"Juliet? Whatever is the matter? Oh, dear, something's happened, hasn't it? Tell me!"

But Juliet didn't have any words left. So, she didn't answer, but buried her face in her sister's shoulder, and burst into tears.

~

"You do realize, Helena, that this entire wretched business started with a plate of tea cakes?" Juliet was sitting cross-legged on an enormous bed in one of Lord Hawke's many bedchambers, a room with heavy beams set deep into towering ceilings, and the largest fireplace she'd ever seen.

Helena was lounging in a nest of pillows beside her, and balanced on a pillow between them was a plate piled high with tea cakes.

"Tea cakes?" Helena paused to consider that, a half-eaten cake in her hand. Mrs. Birt, Lady Fosberry's cook had been keeping Helena well-supplied with them since she'd arrived at Hawke's Run. "No. I don't follow it. Tell me your theory."

Helena was fond of theories. Almost as fond as she was of tea cakes.

Juliet waved one of the offending cakes in the air. "If the scent of Mrs. Birt's tea cakes hadn't lured me into the drawing room the afternoon Lady Fosberry came to Hambleden Manor, I never would have made that dreadful wager, and—"

"If you hadn't made the wager, you and Emmeline wouldn't have gone off to London for the season, and—"

"—and if we hadn't gone to London for the season, we wouldn't have landed in the middle of a disastrous scandal."

Another scandal, that is. Some ladies excelled at singing, others at playing the pianoforte, and still others at tatting lace, or painting on tiny bits of ivory.

The Templetons excelled at scandal.

"It's mortifying that my weakness for such an ordinary confection landed us in the midst of yet another tangle of rumors and lies. It's rather like the city of Troy falling to rubble because of a squabble over a lady's pretty face." Though to give Mrs. Birt her due, her tea cakes were lovely currant and almond ones, sweetened with just a touch of rosewater, and thus not ordinary at all.

Mrs. Birt was a dab hand with the rosewater.

But that didn't excuse Juliet, any more than it did the Greeks or the Trojans. "Blasted tea cakes. It's all their fa—"

"Your theory is flawed." Helena popped the last bit of a tea cake into her mouth, and dusted the crumbs from her fingers. "You would have come to the drawing room to see Lady Fosberry, with or without the tea cakes, and thus would have made the wager and gone to London, thereby setting the scandal in motion."

"I detest it when you pick apart my theories, Helena." Juliet waggled her tea cake accusingly at her sister.

"But think of this, Juliet. If Lady Fosberry hadn't tempted you into the wager with Mrs. Birt's tea cakes, then Emmeline wouldn't be betrothed to Lord Melrose."

"Yes, that's so. Something wonderful did come of that wager, didn't it?"

Lord Boggs had lied about seeing Lord Melrose in London. Lord Boggs, it seemed, couldn't open his mouth without a dozen lies and ugly rumors falling out. He was behind the worst of the gossip about her, too—she was certain of it. It had all been a ploy to make her so desperate she'd agree to become his mistress.

Given she'd sooner toss herself into the Thames, it hadn't worked.

As for Lord Melrose and Emmeline, according to the letter Euphemia had sent Helena, Lord Melrose had pleaded his case so tenderly that Emmeline had succumbed with very little fuss, despite being the stubbornest of all the Templeton sisters.

Their betrothal was the one bright spot in an otherwise unremitting sea of gloom.

Juliet sighed, and helped herself to another tea cake. "Lord Hawke won't be angry that I've come here, will he?"

"Lord Hawke?" Helena snorted. "I haven't the faintest idea whether he'd be angry or not. I haven't laid eyes on the man since I arrived at Hawke's Run."

"But you've been here two months." It wasn't unusual for a nobleman to spend a great deal of time in London, but one would think Lord Hawke might wish to see his sons on occasion. "What of the boys?"

"The boys? Oh, I'm afraid Lord Hawke is far too busy drinking himself into a stupor and chasing ladies of ill repute from one corner of London to the other to spare any time for Adrian and Etienne." Helena seized one of the pillows scattered across the bed, fluffed it with a bit more aggression than necessary, then added it to the stack piled against the headboard. "I'd say it's just as well he kept away from them, but the boys miss him. They ask for him every day."

Juliet's tea cake turned to dust in her mouth. "That's awful, Helena. I'm sorry for them."

"I do my best for them, but those boys need their father."

"They do. All boys do. But Lord Hawke was wise enough to choose you as their governess. That speaks well of him."

"Lord Hawke had nothing to do with it. His housekeeper, Mrs. Norris hired me. I doubt he even knows I'm here."

"Oh, no. Those poor little boys."

"The boys and I go on quite happily without Lord Hawke, I assure you. They've no manners, of course, and the pair of them are as wicked as demons from the underworld, but aside from that, they're dear, lovely little things."

"Dear, lovely little demons? Only you would say such a thing, Helena."

"Indeed, but you didn't come here to talk about Adrian and Etienne." Helena plucked up the plate of cakes and deposited them on a table next to the bed. "What's happened, Juliet?"

That... well, that was a question with no satisfactory answer. There *was* a perfectly foolish, humiliating answer, however. She'd indulged her silly romantic fantasies, hoped for a thing that could never be, and now her heart was broken. "It's quite dreadful, really, Helena. I, ah... well, I've made a terrible mistake."

Her sister said nothing, only waited, a trick she'd picked up from some psychological text of their father's. It never failed to loosen Juliet's tongue. "One can never keep a secret from you, Helena. It's excessively trying."

Helena raised a brow. "You came all the way to Hawke's Run *not* to tell me your secret?"

"It's not as if I came from the other end of England. Steeple Cross is only eight or so miles from here." That wasn't the point, of course, but how did she broach such a subject? One didn't blurt out a thing like this.

"Steeple Cross? What, you mean Lord Cross's estate? I hear the grounds are lovely, though I haven't heard much about Lord Cross himself. Is he—"

"I'm in love with him!" Well. It seemed one did blurt it out, after all.

Helena didn't blink at this outburst, but only regarded Juliet with calm blue eyes. "In love with Lord Cross? Is he—"

"He's awful, Helena! The most stubborn man imaginable—more stubborn than Emmeline, if you can believe it, and then he's terribly arrogant—that is, all earls are arrogant, but he's more so, and he's handsome, like a dark-haired pirate with lovely eyes, but he doesn't smile nearly often enough, which is a great pity, as he has a wonderful smile, and he's... really, Helena, I don't think I've ever encountered a more dreadful man."

"My goodness, Juliet. You *are* in love, aren't you?"

"I am, and I'm terribly disappointed in it. I always imagined falling in love would be rather like... like, well I don't know, exactly—something with rose petals, perhaps—but instead it's like diving into a patch of nettles. They sting, and stick in unmentionable places, and once they've got into you, there's no getting them out again!"

"Yes, that does sound like love."

"What am I meant to do, Helena? How am I ever going to extricate myself?"

"Er, well, perhaps if we approach it scientifically, we can—"

"It is my lady, O, it is my love!"

Helena paused, frowning. "Do you hear shouting?"

Juliet sat up, listening. "It sounds as if it's coming from the garden. You don't suppose the boys have got out, and are running about in the dark?"

"When it comes to the boys, anything is possible." Helena hopped down from the bed, crossed to the window, and peeked through a narrow gap in the draperies. "No. It's not the boys."

"With love's light wings did I o'erperch these walls
For stony limits cannot hold love out."

"Come here, Juliet. There's a man standing in the garden, shouting some nonsense about love."

"That's not nonsense. That's Shakespeare. *Romeo and Juliet*, Act 2, Scene 2, where he sees her on the balcony." But... a man in the garden, reciting lines from *Romeo and Juliet*?

It couldn't possibly be a coincidence, could it? But it must be, unless...

No, surely not.

Juliet stumbled to her feet, hardly daring to move lest she somehow upset the order of the universe, and crossed the bedchamber to the window, her breath held.

"Two of the fairest stars in all the heaven,
Having some business, do entreat her eyes
To twinkle in their spheres till they return."

"What is he wearing?" Helena pushed the draperies aside and squinted down at the garden. "Is that a *red* waistcoat?"

"It's not red," Juliet whispered, her heart thudding against her ribs. "It's scarlet."

"Hmm. So, it is."

His face was turned up to the window, the breeze ruffling his dark hair, and his hand, it was... it was...

A sob escaped her, and she pressed her fingers to her lips.

His hand was over his heart.

"How curious. Why is there a madman in a scarlet waistcoat standing in the middle of the garden, shouting about stars?"

Juliet pressed her palm against the window, her heart in her throat. "That's not a madman, Helena. That's Lord Cross."

CHAPTER
EIGHTEEN

Miles stood in the garden underneath the only lit window at Hawke's Run, his hand over his heart and Romeo's words on his lips, praying he wasn't inadvertently wooing the Earl of Hawke.

"The brightness of her cheek would shame those stars
"As daylight doth a lamp."

Above him the window opened, and a brown-haired lady who was *not* Juliet stuck her head out. "I beg your pardon, Lord Cross, but you're standing on my geraniums."

He jumped backwards, his boot heels sinking into the mud.

"No! Now you've trod on my—"

The window slammed closed. There was a frenzy of movement on the other side of the glass, then another face appeared in place of the first one. The lamplight in the bedchamber behind her cast her features in silhouette, but he knew the curve of her chin, the shape of her lips.

He'd stroked that chin, kissed those lips.

Juliet had come to the window to listen to him. It

wasn't too late, then, to make her see she held his heart in the palm of her hand—that he ached to turn himself over to her, body and soul. He drew in a slow, deep breath, let it out again in a sigh, then opened his mouth to give voice to Romeo's words, and win the heart of *his* Juliet.

But nothing came out. Romeo's speech, every line of it, had evaporated from his memory as quickly as the morning dew at sunrise.

No. This wasn't happening. He just needed to think, to picture the words on the page. He squeezed his eyes closed, but the lines that had been so clear in his mind when he'd left Steeple Cross were now a confusing blur of *thou*, and *thee*, and *wherefore*.

There'd been something about singing birds, and lazy puffy clouds, and... hadn't there been a line about sailing upon the bosom of the air? "Er, mortals that fall back to gaze, and... something, then something else, and... white upturned eyes."

White upturned eyes? That couldn't be right. It sounded like something out of a Gothic horror novel, not a Shakespearean romance.

It had taken him twenty-nine years to find his way to *this* garden, to woo *this* lady. Twenty-nine years, and he was making an utter mess of it. This was going to end with him standing in the mud in a ridiculous scarlet waistcoat, crushed geraniums under his boot heels, shouting nonsense up at a closed window.

Time and time again, words had failed him, but this time, it should have been different. This time, all the words he needed should have been on his lips, waiting for him to breath them into life.

Because this time, it was *her*, and they *had* to be.

He couldn't lose her. Not after he'd taken her into his arms and into his heart.

He stood there, silent, his hand still pressed to his chest as twilight deepened, bathing the garden in a muted golden light, the first stars twinkling in a deep blue sky. And there, at the window above him, *his* Juliet—the only lady who could tint his future with the same golden glow that made twilight so beautiful—was waiting.

And he'd been struck dumb.

Unless... a golden glow and twilit skies twinkling with stars was poetic, wasn't it? Couldn't he simply tell her about that? Couldn't he tell her that every time he thought of her—her dark blue eyes, her grace and wit and kindness, her joyful laugh that caught him square in his chest—she stole his breath?

He'd been writing poetry to her in his head since the moment he met her.

"I, ah... I've never seen eyes as blue as yours, Juliet. Such a deep, pure blue, like oceans and skies, and your smile is a flower bursting into bloom, or... or like the sun cresting the horizon, warming everything it touches, and... and that tiny dimple in your chin drives me mad."

His cheeks grew warm, but he cleared his throat and went on, because the words were all there, right on his lips, and there was no holding onto them any longer, no holding them back.

They were hers. They'd always been hers.

"You're clever, and so brave, Juliet, and... and your voice is like silver bells on Christmas morning, and even when I did everything in my power to forget you, I never could."

She'd gone still, her silhouette framed in the window above.

"I'm in love with you, Juliet. I have been from the start, I just... I didn't know it, because I've never had love before. I didn't believe I ever *could* have it, but you made me wish for something more, and... perhaps you're right about *Romeo and Juliet*, after all. Perhaps it *is* a romance, in a way, although it's... well, I'm willing to discuss it, at least."

He swallowed, waited, his face tipped up to the window. It wasn't Shakespeare, or even poetry, only the incoherent ramblings of a besotted fool.

But it was everything about her that made her who she was to him.

There was a flutter at the window, the evening breeze sighing through the draperies, perhaps, but an instant later the window closed, and the lamp was extinguished. The bedchamber went dark, and the silhouette vanished.

He stood there, staring up at the window where she'd been just minutes before, his heart lost somewhere between soaring in anticipation, and sinking in despair.

What had happened? Had she grown tired of his babbling, and gone to bed, a pillow over her head to drown him out? Has she sent her sister down to scold him about the geraniums? Or were a half dozen large footman about to drag him out of the garden and send him back to Steeple Cross, his heart shattered into—

"It's white upturned *wondering* eyes."

He turned, caught his breath.

She was wearing a white nightdress, a shawl

draped around her shoulders, her hair loose, falling in a dark waterfall down her back. "Wondering eyes?"

"Yes.

'As glorious to this night, being o'er my head,
As is a wingèd messenger of heaven
Unto the white upturnèd **wond'ring** *eyes.'*

THAT SOUNDS BETTER, DOESN'T IT?"

"It does." He swallowed, gazing at her, and whatever she saw in his eyes brought a shy smile to her lips.

She held out her hand to him. "Come with me."

~

THE BEDCHAMBER HELENA had given her was far too grand for the governess's sister, but Mrs. Norris had invited Juliet to choose whichever room she fancied, as the castle was nearly empty.

It was a bedchamber fit for an earl, but Miles didn't look much like the immaculate Earl of Cross tonight. Underneath the scarlet waistcoat, he wore a plain white linen shirt, open at the neck. His thick, dark hair was disheveled, and his cheeks and jaw shadowed with the first traces of an emerging beard.

No flawlessly tied cravat, and no coat.

He looked softer tonight, tousled, the firelight liming his golden skin, catching the shadows at the hollow of his throat and the fine, dark hair on his forearms.

For a moment they stared at each other, then he took a step toward her. "I've never seen your eyes as big as they are right now. You must have known I would come for you, Juliet."

"I didn't know, but I... I hoped you would."

His face softened, and his dark eyes warmed, but he didn't touch her. Instead, he reached into his waistcoat pocket, and drew out a piece of paper.

It was the sketch she'd done of him. He'd found it.

He stared down at the paper before meeting her gaze. "Is this how you see me?"

What a strange question. "It's how you are."

A rueful smile curved his lips. "I'm twenty-nine years old, Juliet, and in those twenty-nine years, not more than four or five people in my life have ever seen me as you drew me."

He seemed to be holding his breath, waiting for her answer, but to her, it was all quite simple. "Then only those few have ever really seen you."

"But you did. You *do*."

"Yes." He'd only ever been one man to her—the man in her sketch.

His large, warm palm settled on her cheek. "Do you... do you want me at all, Juliet?"

"Yes." She didn't hesitate, or make any pretense at ladylike bashfulness. There'd never been a time since their first meeting that she hadn't wanted him.

She'd come to Steeple Cross *for him*.

He slid his hand down her neck, and she shivered at the warm drag of his palm over her heated skin. Her lips parted, and he needed no further invitation than that. His eyes darkened, and with a low groan he urged her closer, into his arms, and his mouth came down on hers.

This kiss wasn't at all like the kiss they'd shared in his study. That kiss had been possessive, hungry, and a little angry, an explosion of passion too long denied. This kiss was slow and sweet, his lips coaxing hers apart with gentle nips and teasing strokes of his tongue.

This kiss was a wooing, a courtship.

How many different kisses hovered on his lips, waiting to be discovered?

A lifetime's worth.

Everything else spun away on a pulse of wild desire the instant his lips met hers, until there was nothing but *him*, his arms around her, his hard chest under her palms, and his kiss, deep and wet.

"Sweet," he whispered, his hot breath caressing her ear, the tip of his tongue dancing along the seam of her lips. It tickled, but not in any way she'd ever felt before.

This tickled *everywhere*. Her lips, the tight tips of her breasts, deep inside her belly, and in the warm, secret place between her legs.

"You're trembling for me, Juliet." He settled his hands at her waist, squeezing gently before sliding them up her rib cage and cupping her breasts in his palms.

Close. So close to where she wanted them...

"I think of you night and day. Your taste." He sucked her lower lip into his mouth, tasting it with his tongue. "The curve of your back." His fingers tripped down her spine. "Your breasts." He dragged a thumb over one of her nipples, his breath leaving his lungs in a rush when her head fell back at the caress.

"Oh!" She gasped as a ribbon of heat wound through her.

"Your sweet, needy little sighs and whimpers." He kissed her, learning all her secrets with his lips, lingering in the places where his kisses made her tremble. His chest rose and fell under her palms as he lavished attention on her neck, the hollow of her throat, the sensitive skin behind her ear.

And his hands, so wicked, his palms cupping her hips, the swell of her lower belly, skimming over the curves of her buttocks, before at last—*at last*—he brought them back to her aching nipples, stroking and circling until she was panting against his neck, then crying out when he pinched one of the taut peaks gently between his fingers.

"Do you like that, love?" He pinched her other nipple, a low, tortured groan dropping from his lips when she jerked in his arms.

Once he discovered what gave her the most pleasure he held her tightly to him, stilling her for his caresses, his teeth scoring her throat as he teased her nipples, alternately pinching and soothing until she was shaking, desire twisting in her belly.

"Miles." She clung to him, her knees weak, her pulse thrumming in her ears, burning for him. "Please."

But there was no need to beg, because he was already giving her everything she ached for. She wrapped her arms around his neck, her shawl falling to the floor at their feet.

"Juliet." Her name on his lips was a whispered breath. "Do you want me, Juliet?" he asked again, just as he had when he'd entered her bedchamber, when the simple warmth of his palm against her neck stole her breath.

She knew what he was asking, understood what would happen between them if she told him she *did* want him, more than she'd ever wanted anything, yet she didn't hesitate—not in her answer, or in her heart.

The word was already there on her lips, just waiting to be spoken aloud. "Yes."

A brush of soft, fine linen skimmed over her ankles, her shins, her thighs, cool air kissing her heated skin as he dragged her nightdress up, up, over the quivering skin of her belly, her stomach, breasts and shoulders until it lay in a white pool beside her shawl.

Then he fell to his knees before her, wrapped his around her waist, and looked up at her, his eyes dark, as dark as night. "Not just for tonight, but for always, Juliet."

"Always." She touched her fingertips to his cheek, then let them drift into his hair, so soft, the thick strands curling around her knuckles. "Yes."

CHAPTER
NINETEEN

M iles closed his eyes at the soft word, and pressed a tender kiss against the gentle swell of her bare belly. She was exquisite, all smooth skin, long, slender limbs, and masses of silky dark hair tumbling over her shoulders.

And she wanted *him*.

He slid his palms up the back of her calves and over her thighs as he rose to his feet. She let out a soft gasp when he scooped her up, cradling her against his chest as he strode to the bed, and laid her gently back against the pillows.

He gazed down at her, his heart pounding in his chest. "You look like a painting."

And she did, a masterpiece, her dark hair like spilled ink against the pure white page of her skin, all her curves laid bare before him, one arm thrown over her head and her nipples—the same lush red as her lips—still pouting from his attentions.

"No, just a woman." Her sultry mouth curved in a half-smile, and she held out her hand to him. "Come here."

He took her hand and brushed his lips over her

knuckles, then released her to shed his waistcoat and shirt before lying down beside her on the bed.

There was no moon tonight, just the muted glow of the firelight playing over her.

He touched a fingertip to her throat, then dragged it slowly down between her breasts, and over her ribcage to her belly, a soft laugh vibrating in his throat when she squirmed beneath his touch. "Are you ticklish?"

There was no reason that should delight him, but it did.

"A little, perhaps." She peeked up at him from under her dark lashes. "May I... may I touch you?"

He caught her hand—he loved her hands, so soft and delicate—and dropped a kiss on her palm. "You can do whatever you like with me." He'd never spoken truer words, and perhaps it should have worried him, how willing he was to turn himself over to her, but for the first time in his life, he wasn't able to hold any part of himself back.

Not from *her*. He never had been, despite all his efforts.

She needed no further invitation, but commenced her exploration of his body without a hint of shyness, as determined in this as she must have been in her studies of Shakespeare, or in practicing her technique at bowls.

"You've got very broad shoulders, my lord," she murmured as she smoothed her hands over them, then trailed her fingers down his neck to his throat, pausing for an instant to touch her fingertip to the hollow there before stroking her palms over his chest.

He caught his breath when her delicate fingers skimmed over his nipples, and her gaze flew to his face, eyes wide. "Oh, is that... should I not touch you there?"

Dear God, she was going to be the death of him with those soft, seeking hands, those wide blue eyes. "No, it's... I like it."

Like it? It was a poor word indeed to describe what her touch did to him.

It was a maddening, delicious torment. Every one of his nerve endings, every inch of his skin was clamoring for her, his breath leaving his lungs in ragged pants, and his cock already as hard as stone, a heavy, demanding weight against his belly, and she'd hardly even touched him yet.

"You're, ah... all this is very...." She dragged her fingertips down his chest to his stomach, pausing when his muscles twitched under her touch. "Sturdy."

He choked out another laugh. "Sturdy?"

"Yes. Much more so than I imagined." Her gaze dropped to his breeches, her cheeks coloring an enticing scarlet at the outline of his hard length pressing insistently against his falls. "Perhaps *virile* is a better word." She caught her lower lip in her teeth, her gaze on his twitching length, and reached out to skim her thumb across the edge of his breeches, her touch leaving a trail of fire across the sensitive skin of his belly.

It was everything he could do not to thrust his hips toward her, beg for her touch, but he sucked in a harsh breath, closed his eyes, and prayed for strength. God, he wanted her hands on him, more than he wanted his next breath, but if those soft palms and clever fingers got anywhere near his aching cock, he was certain to disgrace himself.

He caught her wrist gently in one hand. "Do you mean to say, Miss Templeton, that you imagined me without my clothing?"

"Oh, yes." She looked up at him, the corners of her lips twitching. "Does that make me very wicked, my lord?"

No. It makes you mine.

"Lie back." He urged her against the pillows. "Let me touch you."

She did as he asked, her hair a dark, wild tangle against the white pillows, her eyes a deep, midnight blue. He touched a finger to her chin, tilting her head up so he might take her lips again, plunging his tongue into that warm, slick cavern until breathless sighs and whimpers tore from her lips, and he was struggling not to grind his hips into the bed.

"Do you trust me, Juliet?" He caught a lock of her dark hair between his fingers and brushed it across his lips. "Will you trust me to take care of you?"

"Yes." There wasn't a shadow of doubt in those blue eyes.

She was like a feast laid out before him, with her tight, rosy nipples, and the enticing nest of dark, downy curls between her thighs. He rested a hand on her belly, then leaned over her to press a kiss to the gentle swell. "I want to taste you."

"Taste me?" She blinked down at him.

She hadn't the least idea what he meant, but God, yes, his mouth was watering for her. He wanted her against his tongue, her fingers twisting in his hair as she writhed and moaned for him. He pressed another kiss to her belly, then worked his way up, tracing her bellybutton with the tip of his tongue, then higher, dropping a trail of open-mouthed kisses over her rib cage and in the soft valley between her breasts.

"Oh!" Her hips surged off the bed when he licked one of her nipples. "I can't... that's—"

"Shh. I've got you, Juliet." He cupped her hips in his hands, stilling her, then gave her other nipple a long, wet, stroke with his tongue before closing his lips around the tight bud.

Her hands flew to his head, a needy little cry on her lips. "Ah. That's so... it feels..."

"Does it feel good, sweetheart?" He hovered his mouth over her damp nipple, letting her feel the drift of his breath over the hungry nub. "Do you want more?"

"Ah, *please.*"

He needed no other invitation, but set about devouring her, his hips working against the bed as he gave her what she'd pleaded for, with just the tip of his tongue at first, slow, teasing circles, then more as she grew more frenzied, her hips surging, the sharp tug of fingers in his hair.

Then his hand drifted down, and he slipped it between her legs, parting the delicate flesh and brushing the pad of his fingers over the tight pearl inside. "Open for me, Juliet... yes, that's it," he murmured when she opened her legs to him. "Such a good girl."

He toyed with her nipples, sucking and licking while he stroked lightly between her legs, and God, she was so sweet, the way she gasped and writhed for him that he might have kept it up for hours, holding her at the edge of her pleasure if he hadn't been so desperate to taste her.

He pressed one last, lingering kiss to each nipple

before he drifted lower, kissing his way from her breasts to her stomach, nipping at the soft skin of her belly until he reached the sweet spot between her legs. He settled there, nudging her thighs wider with his shoulders, then burying his face between them, searching out the tiny, throbbing bud with the tip of his tongue.

Her taste, her breathless gasps, the way her thighs dropped open to welcome him tore a groan from deep inside his chest, and he went a little mad then, groaning against her sweet, damp flesh. "Come for me, Juliet. Come, sweetheart... *yes*," he hissed, when she let out a keening cry, and her legs stiffened.

An instant later, nectar flooded his tongue. He lapped at her, eager for every drop, until at last her limbs went loose, and she fell limp against the bed.

He gave her one final, gentle lick before he rose from between her thighs and crawled up the bed, bracing himself on his arms before stretching out on top of her. "So good, Juliet, so beautiful." He brushed the damp tendrils of her hair aside and dropped a kiss on her forehead, still murmuring to her, tender words of praise and desire.

She lay still for a bit, eyes closed and cheeks flushed, but once her breathing calmed, she opened her eyes, and her lips curved in a smile. "Are you still wearing your breeches?"

He glanced down at himself, a wry smile rising to his lips. He was indeed still half-clothed, and his cock stood at such rigid attention, it looked like he'd stuffed a fireplace poker down his breeches. "It, ah... it seems so."

Juliet was already twisting open the buttons on his falls. "Perhaps you should take them off."

There was nothing in the world he wanted more than to tear them off and toss them across the room, but if he did, he'd be tossing his few remaining shreds of restraint aside with them. "Juliet—"

He didn't get any farther, whatever words he'd meant to follow her name dissolving in a deep groan as her hand closed around his length, stroking him. It was hesitant, a little clumsy, her grip too loose, yet it was deeply erotic, the most intense pleasure a woman had ever given him.

Because it was *her*.

He looked between their bodies, mesmerized by the sight of her small hand on him, her dainty fingers wrapped around his rigid cock, and swallowed roughly. "What are... ah, God... what are you doing?"

Her hand stilled at once. "Is this not right?"

It *was* right, more so than anything he'd ever felt before. *Too* right. The kind of right that made a man forget himself, and what he owed to the lady in his bed.

The *virgin* in his bed.

"It's right, but you're... we're not... I'm a gentleman." Good Lord, what a ridiculous statement that was, given he was lying between her thighs right now.

Predictably, Juliet's lips curved in a grin. "Well, it's a bit late for you to remember that *now*, my lord." But then her grin faded, and she reached up to rest her hand against his cheek. "Earlier, you asked me if I wanted you, and I told you *yes*. That hasn't changed, Miles."

He searched her face. There was nothing but desire in those blue eyes, and he wanted her so badly—had wanted her forever, it seemed—but if he truly

ANNA BRADLEY

were the gentleman he claimed to be, he'd leave her
bed and not return until he'd made her his countess.

"I love you, Juliet. I want you to be my wife. We
don't have to live at Steeple Cross, or even Kent. We
can live in London." He'd take her wherever she
asked, wherever she wanted. His home would always
be where she was. "We can go to Buckinghamshire, if
you like, or bring your sisters to—"

"Shh." She touched a finger to his lips. "I'll go
anywhere you are. I love you, Miles," she whispered,
her gaze holding his. "Please."

That was... well, there was nothing more to say,
after that. Every protest dissolved like sugar on his
tongue. He dragged his thumb across her bottom lip,
still reddened from his kisses, then leaned down, and
lost himself once again in her sweet mouth, and the
hypnotizing stroke of her hand against his swollen
cock.

"Open for me again," he whispered, a thrill of
possessiveness shooting through him when she did
as he asked without question, parting her delicious
thighs for his seeking fingers.

He stroked her gently, coaxing her back to wet-
ness before he began opening her to take him,
probing carefully, and clenching his teeth against the
temptation of her tight heat.

He wouldn't hurt her for the world.

So, he held back, stroking and teasing her until a
sigh left her lips, and she grew restless under his
touch. Only then did he take her to the edge with one
teasing caress after another, until she was crying out
for him.

When her fingernails sank into the slick skin of
his back, he tore his breeches off, sent them flying

204

over the end of the bed, and settled between her thighs. "There will be a brief burst of pain, sweetheart. I'm sorry."

She smiled up at him, so lovely and trusting, and shook her head. "I'm not."

As careful as he was with her, she let out a soft gasp when he entered her, and he stilled at once, dropping a kiss on her forehead. "It's over, love."

Yet he waited, hips still, working her sensitive bud until at last she relaxed around him, and gave a tiny, hesitant thrust of her hips. "It's all right, now."

Then he did begin to move in shallow, careful thrusts, his jaw tight with the effort of holding back, but soon enough she was moving with him, her head tipped back against the pillow, lips parted, a wondering expression in her eyes as she gazed up at him.

When she let out a soft cry and wrapped her legs around hips he let go, thrusting deeply into her until they were moving together as one body, one heart. He caught her fevered cries on his lips, breathing his own groans into her mouth as he edged them closer with every plunge of his hips.

He groaned as heat flooded him, pleasure gathering into a tight knot in his spine, but he held back, sweat beading at his temples until at last she let out a cry, and her body pulsed around him, tight and hot, taking him with her into a blissful release.

Afterwards, he tucked her against him, and pressed a tender kiss to her temple. A thousand words flooded his head—all the things he wanted to tell her, a thousand promises he'd make her—but then she sighed against him, her eyelids heavy over her beautiful blue eyes, so he simply held her close.

He had time enough to make her promises, and a lifetime to keep them.

So, he closed his eyes, and they drifted into a deep, dreamless sleep together, his arms wrapped around her, and her hand over his heart.

EPILOGUE

STEEPLE CROSS, EIGHT WEEKS LATER.

"Shame on you, Lord Cross! Is this how you intend to win at bowls? By incapacitating your competitor?" Juliet made a show of trying to disentangle herself from the muscular arms wrapped around her waist, but her husband only urged her closer, his hard chest warm against her back.

"No, this is how I intend to have my way with my beautiful wife." He swept her hair aside and pressed his lips to the curve of her neck, his breath hot against the sensitive skin. "Dear God, you smell good."

"Do I?" She closed her eyes on a soft laugh, her breath hitching when he teased the tip of his tongue behind her ear. The man had the most sinful tongue in all of Oxfordshire.

Maybe all of England.

"Yes. You always do, like sweet cream. You taste like it, too." He buried his face in her hair, inhaling. "I'm weary of bowls, Lady Cross. Surely, there must be *something* else we could do instead?"

She turned in his arms to smile up at him. "You aren't suggesting we abandon our game just so you won't lose to me at bowls again, are you?"

"Certainly not. I would happily lose to you every day." He dragged a finger down the line of her neck, a slow smile rising to his lips when she shivered in response. "No, I'm merely concerned you've had too much sun, and thought we might pursue an, er... indoor activity instead."

"We spent all morning pursuing an indoor activity, my lord, and part of the early afternoon, as well." It had been utterly delightful, too. She'd felt quite decadent, lounging in bed until the sun was high in the sky, laughing with her husband, tracing patterns on his bare chest with her fingertips and whispering in his ear until he'd tumbled her onto her back with a growl, and tormented every inch of her with that wicked mouth.

Indeed, she hadn't the least objection to a return to the bedchamber, only she did so love to tease him, so she might see his lips quirk in that delightful smile that was hers alone.

"But you've had far too much sun, my lady." He trailed his teeth from her earlobe to the corner of her lips. "Your skin is all flushed and rosy."

"It *is* awfully sunny, isn't it?" Indeed, she was beginning to feel quite warm.

If anyone had told her when she first arrived in Oxfordshire all those weeks ago that the sun could shine with such unrelenting cheerfulness over Steeple Cross, she wouldn't have believed a word of it.

But her fears had proved to be unfounded, as there'd been nary a cloud for weeks now. If the delightful weather would only hold for Emmeline and Lord Melrose's visit next week, she'd have nothing else to wish for.

Rain or shine, she had very little to wish for, either way.

All those silly, romantic dreams she'd cherished for so long, well... they were only silly until the moment they came true, weren't they? Somehow or other, the universe had contrived to land her precisely where she was meant to be—in Oxfordshire, at Steeple Cross, with this man, and no other.

It was strange, really, that a man who'd known so little of love himself should have been the means of restoring her own faith in it, but the universe was clever that way, and seemed to know just how to fit two mismatched puzzle pieces together to create a perfect whole.

Now she and Emmeline had only to see to it their three remaining sisters found their own missing pieces, and their own happiness. Euphemia, in particular. Tilly would have a season, and likely set London on its ear when she did, while Helena... well, Helena didn't care a whit for either the season or a husband, but was content to remain as she was.

But Euphemia, well... Juliet sighed. Euphemia was going to be a difficult case, indeed, but she had promised that she and Tilly would come to Steeple Cross for Christmas, so that was something.

"Such a forlorn sigh." Miles tipped her chin up and studied her expression. "Are you thinking of Euphemia again?"

How well he knew her already. "Yes. You must speak to her over Christmas." Surprisingly enough, a rather lively friendship had sprung up between Miles and Euphemia, as if they had an innate understanding of each other. "We must find her as lovely a gentleman as you and Lord Melrose."

"Lovely, am I, my lady?"

"Oh, yes," she murmured. "So very lovely, Lord Cross."

"Then take me to our bedchamber, so I may show you how much I love you." He stroked her cheek with the back of his fingers, his dark eyes tender as he gazed down at her.

"I can hardly refuse, when you look so exceptionally handsome today, my lord." She ran her hands down the front of his chest, over the royal-blue silk waistcoat embroidered with a subtle pattern of intertwining vines done in silver thread. "Has Lord Barnaby given up on the scarlet and gold, then?"

He chuckled. "Barnaby never gives up. No doubt some canary-yellow silk monstrosity bedecked with black embroidered kittens—or worse—is on its way from London even now."

"No, yellow won't do. I don't fancy yellow for you. This shade of blue, however..." she teased her fingers over the tracing of silver vines. "It flatters you, my lord. You quite steal my breath in it. Indeed, it's the perfect blue for you."

"Of course, it's the perfect blue for me, my lady." He caught her hand and pressed a kiss to her fingertips. "It's the same color as your eyes."

Also by Anna Bradley

A WICKED WAY TO WIN AN EARL

A SEASON OF RUIN

LADY ELEANOR'S SEVENTH SUITOR

LADY CHARLOTTE'S FIRST LOVE

TWELFTH NIGHT WITH THE EARL

MORE OR LESS A MARCHIONESS

MORE OR LESS A COUNTESS

MORE OR LESS A TEMPTRESS

THE WAYWARD BRIDE

TO WED A WILD SCOT

FOR THE SAKE OF A SCOTTISH RAKE

THE VIRGIN WHO RUINED LORD GRAY

THE VIRGIN WHO VINDICATED LORD DARLINGTON

THE VIRGIN WHO HUMBLED LORD HASLEMERE

THE VIRGIN WHO BEWITCHED LORD LYMINGTON

ABOUT THE AUTHOR

Anna Bradley writes steamy, sexy Regency historical romance—think garters, fops and riding crops! Readers can get in touch with Anna via her webpage at http://www.annabradley.net. Anna lives with her husband and two children in Portland, OR, where people are delightfully weird and love to read.

ABOUT THE AUTHOR

Anna Bradley writes steamy, sexy Regency historical romance... and riding crops! ... in touch with Anna via her webpage so happy... Anna lives with her husband and two children in Portland, OR, where people are delightfully weird and love to read.